Amy Cross is the author of more than 250 horror, paranormal, fantasy and thriller novels.

OTHER TITLES BY AMY CROSS INCLUDE

1689
American Coven
Angel
Anna's Sister
Annie's Room
Asylum
B&B
Bad News
The Curse of the Langfords
Daisy
The Devil, the Witch and the Whore
Devil's Briar
Eli's Town
Escape From Hotel Necro
The Farm
Grave Girl
The Haunting of Blackwych Grange
The Haunting of Nelson Street
The House Where She Died
I Married a Serial Killer
Little Miss Dead
Mary
One Star
Perfect Little Monsters & Other Stories
Stephen
The Soul Auction
Trill
Ward Z
Wax
You Should Have Seen Her

THE HORROR OF STYRE HOUSE

THE SMYTHE TRILOGY BOOK THREE

AMY CROSS

This edition
first published by Blackwych Books Ltd
United Kingdom, 2024

Copyright © 2024 Blackwych Books Ltd

All rights reserved. This book is a work of fiction.
Names, characters, places, incidents and businesses are
the product of the author's imagination or are
used fictitiously. Any resemblance to actual persons,
living or dead, or to actual events or locations,
is entirely coincidental.

Also available in e-book format.

www.amycross.com
www.blackwychbooks.com

CONTENTS

PROLOGUE
page 15

CHAPTER ONE
page 19

CHAPTER TWO
page 27

CHAPTER THREE
page 35

CHAPTER FOUR
page 43

CHAPTER FIVE
page 51

CHAPTER SIX
page 59

CHAPTER SEVEN
page 67

CHAPTER EIGHT
page 75

CHAPTER NINE
page 83

CHAPTER TEN
page 91

CHAPTER ELEVEN
page 99

CHAPTER TWELVE
page 107

CHAPTER THIRTEEN
page 115

CHAPTER FOURTEEN
page 123

CHAPTER FIFTEEN
page 131

CHAPTER SIXTEEN
page 139

CHAPTER SEVENTEEN
page 147

CHAPTER EIGHTEEN
page 155

CHAPTER NINETEEN
page 163

CHAPTER TWENTY
page 171

CHAPTER TWENTY-ONE
page 179

CHAPTER TWENTY-TWO
page 187

CHAPTER TWENTY-THREE
page 195

CHAPTER TWENTY-FOUR
page 203

CHAPTER TWENTY-FIVE
page 211

CHAPTER TWENTY-SIX
page 219

CHAPTER TWENTY-SEVEN
page 229

CHAPTER TWENTY-EIGHT
page 237

CHAPTER TWENTY-NINE
page 247

CHAPTER THIRTY
page 255

EPILOGUE
page 263

THE HORROR OF STYRE HOUSE

PROLOGUE

2528 BC...

A BRIGHT SHAFT OF sunlight broke through the darkness, illuminating a stone table where two mortuary attendants continued their work on the Pharaoh's body. Proceeding carefully and in silence, the two men were keen to show the greatest respect as they prepared the body for its final resting place.

One of the men picked up a long hooked instrument. He held the tip up and examined it for a moment, checking to make sure that there was no damage, and then he stepped around the table and stopped to look down at the Pharaoh's face. As the other man stepped back, the first attendant leaned down and began to slowly insert the hook into the dead man's left nostril. He knew that this was one of the most delicate parts of the entire procedure, and that any mistake could cause catastrophic damage to the features of the man who – until very recently – had ruled the entire civilization.

But this attendant – a priest with many years of experience – knew exactly what he was doing.

Soon he began to pull the hook out, extracting the first clumps of brain matter. A crunching sound could be heard coming from far back in the nose, but the attendant paid no attention to this as he carefully set the bloodied blobs of meat onto a dish. He glanced briefly at the other man; they'd both already removed the dead king's internal organs through the chest, and they knew that they were now engaged in the most difficult part of their task. Others would soon arrive to judge their work, and any failings would result in instant death. The two men exchanged a worried glance for a moment, and then the first man looked back down and pushed the hook deeper into the nostril.

He worked slowly and cautiously over the next few minutes. Finally, just as he was starting to think that the task was going well, he felt the hook catch on something hidden deep inside the nostril. He pulled gently, then a little harder, only to find that the hook was stuck on what he could only assume was some kind of small protrusion of bone. He turned the handle slightly, trying not to panic, yet the hook still refused to come loose. After looking briefly at his companion, and seeing the fear in the other man's eyes, he returned his attention to the corpse. He knew that there had to be some easy way to get the hook out and continue his work. The nearby plate held a small pile of brain matter, but certainly not enough had been removed just yet. The procedure had to continue, so the man swallowed hard before starting to turn the handle once more.

Telling himself that he could get the hook out from the Pharaoh's nose if only he worked delicately, he turned the hook millimeter by millimeter, and slowly he felt a slight sense of movement, as if -

Suddenly a cat jumped onto the table, knocking the man's arm. The hook ripped out from the Pharaoh's nostril, tearing the side open.

The other attendant lunged forward and grabbed the cat, lifting it up by the scruff of its neck. The first man, horrified by the accident, leaned down and inspected the damage. The hook was still attached to a bony section inside the Pharaoh's nose, but one side of the nostril had been completely destroyed. A moment later a section of bone fell away, causing part of the cheek area to sink down and collapse. Realizing that there was no way to cover up such hideous damage, and that he would surely be executed for disrespecting the Pharaoh in such a manner, the attendant could only stare at first at the immense mess that had been made. After a few seconds, however, he felt his blood begin to boil and he slowly turned to see that his colleague was still holding up the struggling, meowing cat.

Filled now with a rage almost beyond comprehension, the first attendant grabbed a knife from one of the nearby pots. Storming around the table, he approached the cat and looked deep into its eyes, and then he held the knife up and carved the blade across its throat, causing blood to spray from the animal's flailing body even as some of the other mortuary attendants hurried through to find out what was wrong. Ignoring the new arrivals, however, the first man merely let out an angry snarl as he dropped the knife and used his bare hands to rip the dying cat's throat apart, digging his fingertips deeper and deeper into the struggling animal's body as more blood sprayed from the wound and -

CHAPTER ONE

February 1901...

OPENING HIS EYES, SMYTHE found himself staring across the bed at a patch of sunlight that was casting gentle patterns all over the opposite wall. He blinked a few times, but already the details of his latest nightmare were fading away and he remembered only a few scraps about a very angry man and lots of blood.

Turning, he saw that the rest of the bed was empty. Getting to his feet, he looked for a moment at the untidy spot where his mistress had been sleeping, and then he sauntered across the bed before dropping down onto the floor and setting off for the landing.

As he walked, the tip of his tail briefly flicked.

***

"There you are," Lydia said with a smile, not even looking up from her book as she sensed Smythe entering the living room downstairs. "Sorry, I thought I'd let you sleep in. You seemed so tired."

Letting out a faint meow, Smythe brushed against her foot.

"I was up at the crack of dawn," she continued, turning to another page in the book. "The more history I study, the more I see these... throughlines that seem to be part of everything. Ancient Egypt, Ancient Rome... Greece, the Ottoman Empire, the Carpathians... if you know where to look, you can see so many hints of people with these powers. It's certainly not a new phenomenon."

She paused for a moment, fascinated by an image showing some hieroglyphs that had been found in an Egyptian tomb.

"Sometimes I feel like I'm slowly uncovering a tradition that dates back to the time before recorded history," she mused, barely even noticing as Smythe purred and brushed his other side against her leg. "I'm certainly no historian,

Smythe. I just do my best with the books I'm able to get my hands on. Someone who really knew what they were doing, who really had the level of education needed for something like this, would no doubt be able to learn so much more." Sighing, she leaned back as she felt a rush of frustration running through her chest. "Damn it, I wish I could be smarter."

Heading through to his bowl in the kitchen, Smythe looked down and saw just a few scraps of meat. He let out a louder, more distressed meow and turned to Lydia.

"Yes, I know," she sighed, getting to her feet and making her way into the kitchen. "You know, I remember when you hunted for your own food." She took some meat from the side and leaned down to drop it into the bowl, before stroking Smythe's back as he began to eat. "Sometimes I worry that you're becoming a little too domesticated. When we moved into Styre House half a century ago, I thought you'd never run out of rodents to hunt. Esme's pouch of gold and jewels certainly -"

Stopping herself just in time, she felt a shiver run through her chest as she thought back to the last time she'd seen Esme Walker. Sixty-three years had passed since that fateful day when Lydia had left Almsford, but a moment later she caught her own reflection in the glass of a nearby door; in some ways she hadn't aged at all, yet in other ways she could see so much more pain and fear in her own eyes. She thought back once more to Esme standing on that bleak road, and another shiver passed through her body as she reminded herself that there was no point dwelling on the past.

At least, not the *recent* past.

"I'm afraid you're going to have to spend another day alone soon, Smythe," she explained. "There are no two ways about it, I can't continue my research unless -"

Suddenly the window at the far end of the kitchen shattered. Startled, Lydia let out a gasp as she turned and saw a rock landing on the floor amid a shower of tumbling glass. Smythe, meanwhile, had darted away across the room and had stopped to look back from the safety of the doorway.

"Witch!" a girl's voice shouted from somewhere outside, accompanied by the giggles of several other children and the sound of footsteps racing away.

Taking a deep breath and gritting her teeth, Lydia got to her feet and raced across the kitchen. When she reached the window, she looked out through the broken glass just in time to see four young girls running away across the garden. As the other three disappeared around the corner, the fourth girl stopped and turned to her. Lydia recognized this girl as one of the regular troublemakers from the nearby village. She was used to them occasionally harassing her, although this was the first time any of them had been brave enough to actually throw something and cause damage to the property.

"Why don't you fly away on your broomstick?" the girl shouted. "You're nothing but a dirty, smelly old witch!"

"Verity, come on!" one of the other girls yelled from behind the hedge. "If you stop, she'll catch you and turn you into a frog!"

"Witch!" the girl called out again. "Disgusting old hag! How many warts have you got? I bet you're really hideous!"

Filled with a sudden burst of anger, Lydia pulled the door open and stepped outside. The girl, suddenly clearly terrified, turned and raced away, and already Lydia knew that there was no point even trying to shout anything at her.

"Idiots," she said with another heavy sigh. "When will these small-minded buffoons learn that they've got nothing to fear? Even with this provocation, I'd never hurt anyone."

She paused, and once again she thought

back to her past. This time, in her mind's eye, she saw flames engulfing her father's body at the farm.

"Not again," she whispered. "I wouldn't let myself. Those days are..."

Feeling something brushing against her leg, she looked down just in time to see Smythe slipping past and heading out into the garden.

"You've got the right idea," she told him as she watched him approaching the flowerbed. "It's all just water off a duck's back for you, isn't it? I envy you so much, Smythe. I wish my life could be so simple."

Almost as if he'd understood those words, Smythe stopped and looked back up at her.

"It's just you and me now," she continued, feeling a sense of sadness in her chest. "I'm not complaining, I'm just telling it how it is. I'm too dangerous for me to be around other people, and it's not as if I'd ever let anyone touch me anyway. You just seem to get me though, Smythe. I suppose that's one of the best things about having a familiar. You know, sometimes I think you're the only thing keeping me sane. Without you, I'd probably have lost my mind a long time ago. Or lost it more than I already have."

Smythe meowed again, before turning and ducking into the flowerbed, quickly disappearing from sight. Lydia watched as the flowers moved, and then – allowing herself to smile again – she turned and headed back into the kitchen.

After grabbing a towel, she crouched down and started to gather up all the broken glass. She worked methodically and carefully, but after just a few seconds she found her thoughts drifting again. For many years now, she'd been mostly able to put her darker memories aside, yet lately they seemed to be rushing back into her mind. Worried that her past was demanding her attention, she found herself thinking this time about Bloodacre Farm itself, and about the days before her mother had become bed-bound. There had been a period, she had to admit, when her life had been relatively happy. Sure, her father had been a persistent nag, always demanding more attention, but she supposed that was simply what fathers were like with their daughters. She knew of no other way.

At least before finding the old books, Lydia had been fairly carefree, and sometimes she rued the day when her father had gone anywhere near -

Letting out a gasp, she looked down and saw that she'd cut her finger on one of the larger shards of glass. Quickly gathering up the other pieces, she tipped them into the bin and then hurried to the sink. She examined the cut and saw a bead of blood already emerging near the base of her fingernail.

"Damn it," she muttered, as she began to rinse the blood away. "I'm so sorry, Rebecca. You know I wouldn't want to waste any."

Glancing across the counter, she saw the jar that contained a strange mixture of blood and various spices. Once full, that jar was now coming perilously close to running out, and deep down Lydia had known for some time that she was eventually going to have to cook up another batch. The mixture had lasted for more than a decade, but sometimes she could still hear Rebecca Barnett's muffled cries ringing out. Indeed, sometimes she wondered whether those cries had sometimes been bottled in the jar along with so much of the poor girl's blood.

"I've been putting this off for too long," Lydia said under her breath, before turning to look back over at the books in the living room. "There's really no reason to be so scared. I have to make the journey."

CHAPTER TWO

STEAM BILLOWED FROM THE front of the train a couple of days later, as Lydia stepped out of the carriage and stopped to look along the platform at London's Charing Cross station.

For a moment, as hundreds of people milled all around her, she felt as if she had to turn around and head straight home. Clutching her bag, she already knew that she looked like a fish out of water. She was so used to being alone at home, and she absolutely dreaded the thought of being somewhere as busy as London. Almost frozen in place by the fear, she tried to block out the tremendous roar of voices, and she almost succeeded until suddenly she was bumped on the side by a passing man.

"Sorry," he muttered, not even looking back at her as he and the rest of the crowd moved along the platform.

Horrified by the fact that she'd been touched, Lydia took a few seconds to pull herself together. She forced herself to join the crowd, which seemed to move as one huge entity along the platform and out onto the concourse. If she'd intended to go in any other direction, Lydia might not even have been able to push against the flow at all, and soon she found herself walking out to the front of the station. Here, impossibly, the immense sound was even louder, and by the time she reached the side of the road she felt as if she could hear the entire city of London all at once.

Looking around, she saw Trafalgar Square nearby, with Nelson's Column rising up high against the somewhat smoky and dirty sky. Black ribbons had been tied to some of the lampposts, and many people were wearing somber clothing to mark the recent death of Queen Victoria. The sky was hazy with smog rising high across the city.

"Don't worry, Smythe," Lydia said under her breath, thinking of her familiar enjoying himself at home in the peace and quiet of Styre House's garden. "I won't be long. I know exactly what I need to find, and where I have to go to find it."

***

At least the library was a lot quieter than the rest of the city. Having navigated her way through the maze of London's streets, and feeling slightly proud that she'd only once had to stop and ask a policeman for directions, Lydia stood in an dimly-lit aisle and peered at the spines of the various dusty old leather-bound volumes that lined the shelves. Here, finally, she felt a little more like herself again.

Setting her bag on one of the tables, she told herself that at last she could focus on her work.

She reached out to remove one of the books, then at the last moment she hesitated as she realized that she wasn't quite sure where to begin. She only had a few hours before she had to get back to the station for her return train, but there was so much that she wanted to learn. For a few seconds, overwhelmed by so many options, she felt as if a sense of panic might be returning. After a couple more seconds, however, she slid out the book that had been her first choice, and she was immediately surprised by its hefty weight.

"Interesting choice."

Startled, she spun round, dropping the book onto the floor.

"Oh, I'm so dreadfully sorry," the bespectacled man said, hurrying over and picking the book up for her. "That was a close one. If it had landed on your foot, it might have broken your toes."

"I'm sorry," she replied, "I didn't realize that there was anyone else in this section."

"You *did* seem to be in a world of your own," he said with a faint smile. "I should have been more considerate, and for that I can only apologize again." He looked at the book's spine. "Still, it's not often that I see someone pick up a book about myths from the days of the Aztecs. And don't get me wrong, but you don't exactly look like a..."

Hesitating, he looked her up and down for a moment.

"I don't entirely know how to finish that sentence without potentially causing offense," he added. "It's just that you don't look like a... well, a... like a..."

He swallowed hard.

"I'm not a scholar," she told him, hoping to hurry the conversation along a little so that she might be left alone. "I'm just an... interested amateur."

"Nothing wrong with that," he countered.

"Sometimes the self-taught can discover insights that the rest of us gloss over." He paused, clearly feeling somewhat uncomfortable. "I'm trying to be complimentary," he added, reaching a hand out toward her, "but I'm not sure that I'm doing very well. My name is Jimmy. James Ward, actually, I'm the head researcher in the library. Please, if you have any questions at all, you mustn't hesitate to come to me. And call me Jimmy."

"Absolutely," Lydia replied, before looking down at his outstretched hand. "I, uh..."

The thought of touching anyone's hand left her feeling utterly horrified, but she knew that she had no choice. Taking his hand and giving it a gentle shake, she tried very hard to avoid wincing and to hide the fact that she was worried she might be about to throw up.

"And your name is..."

"Lydia," she said, before she had a chance to wonder whether she should tell the truth at all. "Lydia Smith."

"Welcome to our humble library, Lydia Smith," he said, seemingly quite flustered now. "I'm going to leave you alone so that you can get on with your work, but please don't forget what I told you." Letting go of her hand, he took a step back. "I'm at your disposal while you're here with us at the library, but don't worry. I'm pretty good at knowing when to appear and when to disappear. I won't trouble you."

He paused, before remembering to hand the book back to her.

"Thank you," she replied, and she felt hugely relieved as he turned and stepped out of view. She listened for a moment to the sound of his footsteps heading away into the distance, and then she looked down at the book in her hands. "You've been most kind."

Yet again, she found herself having to really focus her thoughts. Carrying the book to a nearby table, she was about to sit down when she realized that she'd left her bag on one of the shelves; she hurried over and retrieved the bag, and then – as she headed back to the table – her left foot caught on a chair and she fell. Landing hard on her knees, she let out a faint gasp that seemed so much louder in the cavernous silent library. Looking around, terrified that she might have attracted more attention, she was relieved to find that there was nobody in sight.

And then, as she began to get to her feet, she winced as she felt a faint pain in her knees.

Ever since she'd rejuvenated her body a few years earlier, Lydia had been caught between youth and old age. She knew that the potion had rolled back the years and had made her younger, yet at the same time she also worried that her mind was struggling to keep up. Now even her knees were straining, but she knew that more of the potion would hopefully fix any problems. She was running out, but she'd made some once before and soon she'd simply have to bite the bullet and do the same thing again. Reaching out, she supported herself against a table as she slowly hauled herself up, and finally she managed to maneuver herself onto one of the seats.

Hearing footsteps, she looked over her shoulder, terrified that someone might approach. She saw a woman walking past the end of the aisle, but the intruder was soon gone. Still, Lydia felt increasingly paranoid, worried that someone might be watching her from some hidden vantage point. She glanced around, trying to spot any gap that might reveal a glaring eye on the other side, and several minutes passed before she felt truly at ease. The idea of somebody seeing her, of someone perhaps working out what she was up to, filled her with absolute terror and dread.

Opening the book, she began to search for the relevant chapter. Once she'd found the section she was after, she began to read and all her fear evaporated. Indeed, she almost forgot about the rest of the world as she found herself drawn into descriptions of ancient customs that seemed at once both strange and familiar. Strange because they came from a different place, from a world that had died out hundreds of years ago, but familiar because in some way she was growing ever more aware of a common thread that stretched across the centuries.

Indeed, the more she read, the more Lydia felt as if she was edging closer and closer to some great and very profound revelation about her powers.

CHAPTER THREE

"I'M AFRAID YOU'LL HAVE to take the train from platform two that leaves at three minutes past the hour," a ticket attendant was explaining to a woman at Charing Cross, "and then change for the line along to Canterbury."

Sitting at a small cafe near the concourse, and trying to drown out all the voices around her, Lydia focused instead on everything she'd learned at the library. Having originally intended to only spend a few hours in the city, she'd ended up going through book after book until closing time; even now there were many more volumes that she knew she should have checked, and she was already contemplating the horrific idea that she might actually have to return to London soon. She took a sip of tea, but a moment later she became aware of a figure stepping over to her table.

"Are you alright there, M'am?" the attendant asked.

"I'm quite fine, thank you," she replied politely.

"Are you traveling alone?"

"I am," she told him, "but I know the time of my train."

"If you need escorting to the platform, I -"

"Just because I'm not accompanied by a husband," she replied, cutting him off, "doesn't mean that I'm helpless." She paused, aware that she'd been a little unfair to the man. "Please accept my apologies," she added. "I just mean that I can find my way around. I'm sure there are other people who are far more in need for your assistance."

"Of course, M'am," he said, forcing a smile. "I didn't mean to imply otherwise. Make sure to get to your platform in good time, though. The trains don't wait for latecomers."

"Yes, I know that too," she said under her breath, and then she felt relieved as the man made his way off to speak to other passengers.

Taking a deep breath, she told herself that there was no need to get quite so upset whenever she had to speak to a stranger. Indeed, as she looked across the concourse and saw the high arched glass roof, she actually began to feel rather pleased with herself for managing the journey without incident. She tried to imagine how either of her parents would have fared in the same situation, and she knew without a shadow of a doubt that they'd both have been utterly lost in London. They'd also have been horrified by the idea of a woman traveling alone, but then again she knew that both her mother and father had belonged to an era that was now long gone. And in that moment, Lydia felt as if she was truly a very modern woman.

And an Edwardian, to boot. After all, the Victorian age had died with the late queen, and her son Edward was now ushering in the new century. Even Lydia could feel a sense of change in the air.

"There you are!"

She turned to see Jimmy, the young man from the library, rushing toward her table. Before she had a chance to ask what he was doing, she saw him set her bag down.

"You left this behind," he said breathlessly. "I found it after closing time and, well, I remembered that you'd been carrying it earlier."

"You're most kind," she replied, pulling the bag closer, shocked that she could have left something so important at the library.

"Your train ticket is still in there," he told her.

"That is a relief," she said, realizing that she would also have been unable to pay for her cup of tea if the bag hadn't been returned. "I can't thank you enough."

"I had to do a little detective work to reunite you with your property," Jimmy explained, and now he was starting to get his breath back. "I asked Mr. Simmons on the front desk about you, and he remembered you arriving. He was able to pull up your membership card, and that had your address on it. I supposed that you were probably heading back on the train today, and that meant you'd have to be leaving from Charing Cross. So I raced here just as fast as possible, and you can't imagine my relief when I found you sitting here."

"I am indebted to you," she told him. "I'm really not quite sure what I would have done if I had discovered that I'd left my bag behind. I'd have had to return to the library, but if it was shut... Well, I would have been in a very difficult situation."

"Oh, I'd have waited for you," he replied. "I'd have assumed that you were coming back, and I would have sat there all night if necessary."

"You're really too kind."

"All part of the service," he explained,

before a somewhat uncomfortable silence fell between them. "I don't mind working late, anyway," he added finally. "Sometimes I even stay behind to do a little of my own research. I'm something of a history aficionado, you see. I love rooting through all the different facts and stories from the past, trying to work out what's true and what isn't."

Lydia offered what she hoped would be taken as a polite smile, but not one designed to encourage further conversation.

"It's astonishing how one tale can be related in so many different ways, isn't it"? Jimmy continued. "Two tellings of the same story can have so many different details. But as a historian, we have to try to find ways to cut through it all and get to the truth. And I'm convinced that the truth is always there, waiting to be discovered if we just stick to the task."

"Indeed," she said, before glancing at the clock and seeing that the time had almost come to pay for her tea and go to the platform. "I just -"

"My area of interest is local history," he told her, cutting her off before she could say another word. "Some might find that boring or dry, but to me it's fascinating. If you happen to be coming up to the library again at any point soon, I'd be more than happy to arrange a little meet-up so that I can show you some of the things that I've been working on."

"Oh, that's very kind," she replied, getting to her feet, "but I really don't come to London very often at all."

"I get that," he said with a sigh. "It's so busy, isn't it?"

"I'm used to a quieter life," she explained, glancing at the counter and seeing that there were no customers there now. "And now, if you'll excuse me, I must go and pay. I really don't want to miss my train. But thank you so much for bringing my bag, I honestly don't know what I would have done without it."

"Of course," he said, clearly a little disappointed that she was leaving already.

Smiling again, Lydia turned and headed toward the counter, although she quickly realized that Jimmy was hurrying to catch up to her.

"I can walk you to the platform, if you like," he said. "I'd feel bad not doing that."

"There's no need," she told him.

"But I'd like to," he continued, as she stopped and paid her bill. "It really wouldn't be any trouble at all."

"I'm sure you have far more important things to be doing," she replied, turning to him once she was done. "Sir, I must thank you yet again for your kind help, not only here at the station but also at the library. However, I made it all the way up here to London by myself, and I am quite sure that the return journey will be no trouble either. If I have reason to come to the library again, it will be most pleasant to see you, but I am no historian. I am merely a... keen amateur."

"Sometimes those are the best kind," he replied, although he seemed a little dejected now

"Thank you again," she said calmly. "I wish you a pleasant onward journey to wherever you're going this evening."

Jimmy opened his mouth to reply, but he couldn't get any words out and instead he felt utterly powerless as he watched Lydia walking away. Letting out a sigh, he knew that there was no point running after her, and he told himself that he'd simply have to accept that he probably wouldn't ever see her again. At the same time, as he watched her disappearing into the crowd, he couldn't help but marvel that such a young-looking woman was able to navigate her way around the city without any assistance whatsoever.

"The modern world is a perplexing place," a voice said, and Jimmy turned to see that a ticket attendant had wandered over. "I tried to help that lady, but she insisted that she knew where she was going. She seemed to become rather prickly."

"Indeed," Jimmy said wistfully.

"That's probably why she doesn't have a husband," the attendant continued, lowering his voice a little. "I honestly don't know what's going to become of the world. Then again, I suppose I might be old-fashioned." He paused for a moment. "She seems to know her way around, which isn't bad for someone of her young age."

"Indeed," Jimmy said again, before taking Lydia's library card from his pocket and looking at the details. "Then again, I suppose she's not doing too badly for someone who's supposedly eighty-one years old."

"Eighty-one?" the guard replied, chuckling as he turned to go and assist some other travelers. "She's no more than twenty-two or twenty-three at most."

"I know," Jimmy said, briefly spotting Lydia as she made her way onto the platform, then losing her once again in the crowd. "Perhaps there has simply been a clerical error." He paused again. "Then again, her choice of reading material today at the library was *most* unusual..."

CHAPTER FOUR

"OH, I'M EXHAUSTED, SMYTHE," Lydia said as she leaned back in her favorite armchair a few hours later, taking a little rest before bed. "Truly exhausted. I hate to admit any kind of defeat, but I really don't think that I can go to London again. That place is just so terrifying."

Smythe jumped up onto her lap and settled down so that Lydia could stroke him gently.

"Then again," she continued, "I hear that there are places in the world that are even busier. When I read of a city such as New York or Paris, for example, I wonder whether I would even be able to breathe in such vast crowds. I might be a little old-fashioned, but I'm not sure that it's good for people to live that way. I worry for the future if we continue upon this path as a species." She thought for a moment, imagining a far-off world filled with huge crowds and unbelievable machines. "Then again," she whispered, "perhaps nobody can fight the future. We only -"

Before she could finish, she heard the unmistakable sound of footsteps on the gravel outside. Smythe immediately jumped from her lap as she got to her feet and walked over to the window. Opening the door, she stepped out onto the decking and stopped next to the makeshift 'Smythe House' sign that she'd once hung up for a little joke. She looked across the pitch-black garden, yet although she saw no sign of an intruder, she felt absolutely certain that somebody was nearby.

"Who's there?" she called out. "This is private property and you must leave immediately."

She waited, and after a few seconds she realized that she could sense just the slightest hint of movement somewhere nearby. She turned and looked toward the old garage at the far end of the garden; caught in a haze of moonlight, the garage looked completely untroubled yet Lydia was starting to feel that somebody was lurking in its shadows. Sometimes she wondered whether her unusual powers gave her a small advantage in such matters, although at other times she supposed that all people probably had at least some degree of instinct. The more she watched the garage, however, the more she began to suspect that somebody was indeed hiding, and after a few seconds she was suddenly struck by a moment of clarity.

A child.

The intruder was a child.

Realizing that this must be one of the children who'd thrown a rock through her window a few days earlier, she felt a ripple of anger. Quickly, however, she understood that she needed to frighten the intruders so that they would never bother her again.

Hearing a meowing sound, she turned to see Smythe watching her from inside the house.

"You wait there," she told him, gently shutting the door before stepping off the decking and heading out across the garden, making her way toward the garage.

Already she could sense a heartbeat nearby. Multiple heartbeats, in fact.

"So you've come to see the witch, have you?" she called out, determined to make herself seem as frightening as possible."You're brave, I'll give you that, but also very foolish. You must know that there are others who have made the same mistake, and what do you think happened to them? Hmm?"

Stopping in front of the garage, she realized that the heartbeats were getting faster now. She was picking up a trace of four of them, which made sense since she'd seen four children sneaking onto her property in the past. Part of her hated them for intruding, but at the same time she tried to remind herself that they were only children and that they really didn't know any better. The fact that they were children, however, meant that she felt scaring them wouldn't be very difficult at all.

"You should run while you still can," she continued. "What are you doing out so late, anyway? Do your parents not wonder where you are? Can't you be -"

Suddenly she heard a scrabbling sound, and she turned just as four young figures raced out from behind the garage.

"Witch!" one of them shouted, but already the children were running away from the house.

Lydia opened her mouth to call after them and try to scare them again, but at the last second she heard a gasp, followed by a thudding sound, and then by a cry of pain. She waited, furrowing her brow, and a moment later she realized that she could now hear someone sobbing in the darkness.

***

"What's your name?" Lydia asked, as she soaked another cloth in warm water and prepared to finish cleaning the girl's grazed knee. "It's alright. You can at least tell me your name, can't you?"

Looking up at the girl, she saw true terror in

her eyes. The girl seemed almost frozen in place, as if – since being helped into the house – the poor thing could barely even think straight.

"My name is Lydia Smith," she continued, hoping to perhaps establish some kind of connection. "I live here all alone." Hearing a meowing sound, she glanced over her shoulder and saw Smythe watching from the doorway. "Well, alone except for my cat Smythe." She turned to the girl again. "Smythe is my constant companion. He's my -"

She stopped herself just in time, before the word 'familiar' could leave her lips.

"Well, he's my friend," she added. "Smythe and I have had some adventures together, that's for sure. Now, I really should clean the rest of this wound. You took such a tumble running around out there in the dark. I think your friends might have gone back to the village without you, which is rather mean of them." She began to wipe some more grit from the wound. The girl let out a pained gasp but otherwise remained still. "It's very late. Your parents must be worried about you."

"That hurts!" the girl hissed.

"There's no way around that, I'm afraid," Lydia said as she picked out a particularly large clump of dirt. "The side of your leg is red raw. You were limping heavily when I brought you inside. Do you want to get up and see if you can walk?"

She pulled back and watched as the girl tried to lift herself up from the chair. For a few tantalizing seconds success seemed near, but finally the girl cried out again and dropped back down into the chair as if the pain was too much.

"Let's hope you haven't done any permanent damage," Lydia told her. "We're going to have to get you home, though. You can't stay here, for various reasons."

"I don't *want* to stay here," the girl replied, her voice tense with fear. "You're a..."

"Yes?"

"You're a witch."

"Am I?"

"Everyone knows it," the girl continued. "There was even a meeting last month at the parish church, everyone went, even my father. They were talking about you, and about how they don't want you living here."

"I've never done anything to them," Lydia countered, unable to shake a sense of dread. "There's no reason whatsoever for them to fear me."

"They've heard rumors," the girl said. "People say that you came here a long time ago, and that before you arrived you did bad things somewhere else."

"Has anyone been more specific about those bad things?" Lydia asked.

"Did you kill Rebecca Barrett?" the girl

replied. "They said you killed her a long time ago and took over her body."

"I see," Lydia said, before rolling her eyes. "I *did* know Rebecca, but I certainly haven't taken over anyone's body. Rebecca and I had a... brief association, we didn't know each other very well, and then... I really don't want to get into it, but I know people have been whispering ever since." She paused. "As I explained, this isn't the right time to discuss such matters," she added, standing up. "We're simply going to have to get you home, and I'm afraid you'll need my help for that, so you have no choice. We're not -"

In that instant, she spotted a face in one of the windows. She saw her own reflection, and that of a ghostly figure standing right behind her, glaring at her with dark dead eyes. Turning, she half expected to see the dead face again, but to her relief there was no sign of anyone. Looking back down at the girl in the chair, she told herself that she had to deal with one problem at a time.

"Come on," she said, holding out her hand. "Let's get you home. Believe me, I don't much savor the thought of a walk through the night either, but you can't stay here. Or do you want to wait around with me?"

Ignoring Lydia's outstretched hand, the girl tried again to get to her feet. She let out a cry of pain and almost fell, but at the last second she instinctively reached out and grabbed Lydia's hand.

"This is going to take a while, Smythe," Lydia said, supporting the limping girl as they headed very slowly toward the back door. "Don't wait up." She looked down at the girl again. "Oh, and her name was Rebecca Barnett. Not Barrett. My friend's name, all those years ago, was Rebecca Barnett."

CHAPTER FIVE

ALMOST THREE HOURS LATER, having slowly shuffled along winding country roads in the darkness, Lydia finally knocked on the front door of a small stone cottage at the edge of the village. She waited, and soon enough she heard the sound of footsteps approaching the door's other side.

"Mother will be so angry with me," the girl whimpered, clearly dreading what was going to come next. "I'm in so much trouble."

"I'm sure it'll be fine," Lydia told her. "Your mother is probably overcome by worry, and she'll merely be glad to find that you've made your way -"

In that instant the door flew open, and a furious woman stormed out onto the step.

"Verity Cain, where have you been?" the woman snarled, grabbing the girl's arm and pulling her forcefully into the house. "What are you doing running around at all times of the day and night, when you should be tucked up in -"

Gasping as more pain burst through her leg, Verity slumped down onto the floor.

"You stupid little thing," the woman sighed, before turning to Lydia. "Where did you find her? What -"

Stopping suddenly, the woman stared at Lydia with a horrified expression, before taking a step back.

"It's *you*!" she stammered.

"Your daughter and some of her friends came to my home tonight," Lydia said firmly. "They've been causing a lot of trouble for me lately, and I'd really rather that it all stopped. Would you mind keeping control over her from now on? She injured herself while she was running away, and I fixed her up as best I could but -"

Before she could get another word out, the door slammed shut in her face. Shocked, Lydia stood in silence as she heard a scrambling sound coming from inside the cottage.

"What were you doing out there?" the woman shouted, as a series of cracking sounds were followed by the young girl crying out in pain. "You brought that witch straight to our door! Wait until your father hears about all this!"

"You're welcome," Lydia said softly, before

turning and heading away from the cottage.

Stopping by the side of the road, she took a moment to look toward the church at the far end. She'd very rarely visited the village, preferring to make do with what she could grow and forage out near her own home, and she had to admit that being back in a small community felt very strange. The village was certainly nothing like London, but it seemed busy and overwhelming in its own strange way, and she couldn't help but think back to her time living near Almsford. A shiver ran through her bones as she remembered Robert Potter and Esme Walker and all the other awful people she'd encountered back then, and then she recalled the sight of her own dying mother being carried to the riverbank. People, she felt, were always bad news.

Hearing the door opening behind her, she turned to see the woman stepping back out.

"I hope young Verity will be alright," Lydia said, "and that -"

"Get out of here!" the woman yelled, throwing a bucketful of cold water over her before turning and hurrying back into the cottage. "We're good, honest people! You have no right to be here bothering us!"

"I was trying to help your daughter," Lydia gasped, soaked now as she took a step back. She watched as the door slammed shut, and then she let out a heavy sigh. "I didn't do anything wrong! It's not my fault you can't control your own children!"

***

At least the walk home didn't take three hours. No longer burdened by the need to support a limping child, Lydia managed to reach Styre House in little over one hour. Exhausted, she stopped as she reached the bottom of the steps that led up into the garden, and for a moment she felt as if her tired legs might not be able to carry her to the front door.

A meowing sound let her know that Smythe was nearby, and sure enough a moment later he hurried down to greet Lydia by brushing against her legs.

"This has been quite a day," she said, before turning and looking across the fields. "Sometimes I think that nobody's supposed to live for this long, Smythe. The longer I go on, the more I feel as if the world is becoming this huge mess that's simply impossible to understand."

Smythe let out another meow.

"Apparently they've been having meetings about me," she continued, watching the darkness and imagining the sleepy little village waiting out there in the night. "They've been in their little church, nattering away about what they should do with me. I've done nothing to them, I've left them alone, but it's not enough. They're angered by my mere existence." She paused as the anger continued to spread through her body. "I could wipe their stupid homes away in an instant," she added through gritted teeth, "and leave the ground salted so that nothing could ever grow there for a million years. I could turn them all to dust, and I could do it slowly so that they feel every excruciating second."

Her bottom lip was trembling now as she began to wonder why she didn't just do all of that. For a moment she felt sorely tempted to teach them a lesson, and to demonstrate the immense power that lay within her body. She knew that she'd barely tapped even one thousandth of that power, and sometimes she found herself contemplating what might happen if she just let it all out in a moment of infinite rage.

She knew she could destroy the village.

She knew she could possibly even destroy the entire county.

Could she, she wondered now, destroy the whole world? She began to contemplate that possibility. She knew she'd have to start with the local village, that she'd peel the flesh from their miserable bodies and make them scream, that she'd draw prayers for mercy from their lips before finding unimaginable new ways to hurt them. Then she'd start ripping up the ground, hollowing out the county, before turning her attention to London. The idea of ripping that wretched metropolis of sin and smog apart filled her with so much glee that she began to feel an almost orgasmic urge to rain fire and destruction down upon the land. England, she supposed, could be destroyed within minutes, and then she'd be able to spread the flames of her anger all around the world, burning away every last judgmental fool who could pose a threat. And then, finally, she could live alone in the ruins of the world with just Smythe for company, and she knew she might actually be happy.

Smythe meowed again.

Startled from her fantasy, she looked down and realized that she'd inadvertently clenched her fists. A moment later she spotted flames nearby, and she turned to see that some plants in an old stone pot had begun to burn. Horrified by the realization that her fantasy had begun to seep out, she quickly extinguished the flames and then took a series of deep breaths.

"No," she said softly, "I can't ever do anything like that. I could never live with myself."

Turning and heading inside, with Smythe following, Lydia was careful to lock the front door properly. She had no idea how long she'd spent on her feet, but all she could think about now was that she wanted so desperately to climb into bed and sleep peacefully until morning. She had no clue what the next day might bring, of course, and as she trudged up the staircase she couldn't help but worry that the people from the village might hold another meeting about her in their church, and that eventually one of these meetings might cause more trouble. This particular village had no ducking stool – she'd been *very* careful to check that fact before buying Styre House in the first place – but as she reached the door to her bedroom she knew that humans had no limit when it came to causing trouble.

And then, hearing a creaking sound coming from one of the other bedrooms, she turned and looked across the landing. Sure enough, she heard the sound again, and she realized that the spare bedroom was starting to show its age. She hesitated, dearly wanting to just retire for the night, but finally she crossed the landing and pushed the opposite door open, and then she looked into the darkened room just as another creaking sound rang out from elsewhere.

Behind her, Smythe meowed again.

"No, Smythe," Lydia said, as tears began to fill her eyes, "I'm not scared of ghosts. Not for one second." She turned to him. "I'm sure everything will be alright. We just have to keep the faith for a little while longer."

CHAPTER SIX

FOOTSTEPS ECHOED ALONG THE library's aisle as, one week later, Sir Maximilian Withers came to the end of his customary circulatory perambulation around the facility. Puffing on his pipe, Withers spotted a familiar figure sitting at the desk near the foot of the grand staircase, and with a chuckle he made his way over and looked down at the assorted books that had been laid out.

"Busy, are you?" he muttered, taking another puff on the pipe. "Mr. Ward, you really are the most inquisitive fellow I've ever met in my life. What are you reading about now?"

"I'm sorry," Jimmy replied, leaning back in his chair. "I hope you don't think that I'm spending too much time on personal projects. All my work for the morning is done and I'm just waiting for -"

"Don't worry about any of that," Withers replied dismissively, before leaning down to get a better look at one of the books. "What's this all concerning, anyway?" he asked. "Who's Margaret Marston when she's at home?"

"That's just it," Jimmy said, "I don't really know. There's a Maggie Marston and a Mary Marston and a Margaret Marston, not to mention two Margaret Manstons, and trying to nail down the truth is very difficult. They might all be the same woman, or they might be five different women, or they could be some combination. I'm just trying to work out which, if any, of them lived in a village called Almsford about sixty-something years ago."

"Is this more of your... what do you call it again? Social history?"

"I've always been fascinated by some of the local folklore from the region," Jimmy explained, "and this Marston woman's name has cropped up on so many occasions. By the end of her life, she was known as Old Mother Marston and there were so many rumors about her. One that always caught my attention was the idea that she was somehow the guardian of a set of very old and powerful books that had been handed down through many generations. To be honest, I've been trying to track those books down for a long time. Some people even claim that they were bound in leather from human victims. I'd love to know the truth. Not because I believe all the claims about them, of course, but because from a historical point of view it's fascinating to see how these myths and legends are spread from one generation to the next."

"It is?"

"You can tell a lot about a society by studying these things," Jimmy suggested.

"You can?"

"You can tell a lot about people," he added, "by seeing what they choose to get angry about."

"Really?"

"It's complicated."

"It certainly seems to be," Withers muttered, examining the state of his pipe for a moment before taking yet another puff. "I'm going to leave you to it, but I certainly hope you find this woman. She's long dead now, I assume?"

"Oh, yes," he replied, "and to be honest, I'd more or less given up on the idea of ever making any progress. Then this woman showed up last week at the library and a few things about her grabbed my attention. I was too busy until now to really get into it, but I'm wondering whether the whole thing is linked to some other rumors from the same village."

"You're not going to disappear down some strange rabbit hole of theory and counter-theory, are you?" Withers asked, raising a skeptical eyebrow. "I'd hate to see you lose focus on your more valuable and important work."

"Don't worry," Jimmy said, "this is strictly a side project. I'm merely curious, that's all. You know me, Sir. I'm very much a reader. I'm certainly the last person who'd ever get his hands dirty with anything like this."

***

"I'm glad to see a good turnout here," Martin Compson said as he stood at the front of the parish church, watching the two dozen villagers who'd shown up for the hastily-arranged gathering. "Of course, I'd like to have *everyone* with us today, but I suppose one can't be too greedy. The others simply don't comprehend the nature of the danger that lurks in our midst."

"Is it true?" Alice Waddell asked, her voice trembling with fear. "Did the witch out at Styre House try to snatch young Verity Cain?"

"The details are obscure," Martin replied calmly, "but Verity's mother fears that the witch attempted to lure the child to her doom. We must all give extra thanks for her safe return."

"It's a miracle," one of the other men muttered, shaking his head darkly. "There's no other word for it. It's an absolute miracle."

"We can't rely on miracles forever," Martin said firmly. "There comes a point when we have to take matters into our own hands. I want to make this very clear to everyone gathered here this morning. We have a witch living in our home, and her evil is only going to spread. She must be -"

"What about Rebecca?" another voice asked.

"I was about to get to that point," Martin continued. "A little over ten years ago, poor dear Rebecca – daughter of Edward and Elizabeth Barnett – vanished, never to be seen again. There has been no trace of her since, but we all know that the witch had something to do with her disappearance. I'm not going to pretend to you for one moment that I know exactly what the witch did to Rebecca, but the truth will come out eventually. We cannot allow another of our children to be killed by such an unholy monstrosity."

"Then what do you propose we do about it?" David Overton asked, getting to his feet. "We've talked endlessly about Lydia Smith but I haven't seen anyone actually *do* anything about her."

A general murmur of agreement spread through the congregation.

"We can't just take the law into our own hands," a man in the far corner suggested.

"On the contrary," Martin replied, "that's exactly what we must do. We can't wait for someone from the outside to come and save us, or for divine intervention to deliver us from this evil. That's why I propose that after this meeting ends, any men who are interested in taking action should remain behind so that we can debate our next step. There's no need for the entire community to be burdened with the task. A small group would be much better suited to our needs."

He paused, watching the congregation and hoping that that his words were starting to sink in; he already knew that there were at least half a dozen men who could be relied upon to join him in his crusade.

"The rest of you must put this out of your minds, as best you can. Look after your children and keep them safe. And let me promise you that this is the last time we'll ever have to meet in this manner. The witch will soon be gone."

As the crowd began to leave the church, Martin stepped down from the pulpit. Already several men had made their way over to loiter uncomfortably, waiting for the rest to depart.

Several more minutes passed, until finally Martin found himself with ten other men who were evidently ready to take up the fight.

"Alright, then," David Overton muttered once they were alone. "Let's not drag this out. We need to get it over with. What's the plan?"

"First," Martin replied, "I need assurances that our discussions will go no further. There are people in this village who'd try to get in our way if they ever discovered what we're planning I'm happy for evidence to be presented to the others after the fact, but we can't let anyone interfere until we're done."

"Fine by me," another man suggested. "There's already been more than enough talk about this situation. If we don't act now, that witch is going to cause more trouble."

"They say she's never aged," a fourth man added.

The others turned to him.

"I don't know how true that is," he continued, "but... I mean, it's what everyone says. I even heard that she drinks the blood of innocent girls so she can live forever."

"Is that what happened to Rebecca?" David asked.

"It might well be," Martin replied, "but if that's the case, then it's our job to make sure that she shall be the witch's last victim. Ten years and more have passed since her certain death, and I'm sure Lydia Smith is positively itching to kill again. One way or another there has to be a death around here soon, and it's just up to us whether we want the victim to be a member of our village or..."

His voice trailed off for a moment.

"I think," David said cautiously, "that we all know what we have to do."

"So let's get on with making our plans," Martin said firmly. "Gentlemen, time's wasting and we're not getting any safer. It's time for us to put our heads together, and then we have to go out to Styre House and kill the witch."

CHAPTER SEVEN

STANDING AT THE SINK, with morning light streaming through a few drops of rain that had fallen during the night, Lydia looked out at the sunlit garden and felt something that seemed completely alien.

Peace.

Just for one moment, really only for a few snatched seconds, she felt utterly at peace with herself and with the world. She knew that would change soon, of course, and that she didn't even *deserve* to feel such peace. All her worries and fears and regrets would soon come rushing back, but for a brief stolen moment – almost separate from time itself – she allowed herself to know how it felt to be truly content.

Hearing a gentle meow, she turned to see

that Smythe was entering from the garden.

"There you are," she said with a faint smile. "I've finished all my usual tasks for the morning. Now I have to write down some notes about my recent research. I feel I'm really building toward something, Smythe, but I can't afford to hold back now. Whatever Old Mother Marston was doing with those books, it's almost as if she was searching for something and I'm somehow continuing that work." She sighed. "I know how foolish that sounds, and I might well be deluded, but I can't shake the sense that what I'm doing is in some manner... important."

Smythe stared at her for a moment longer, before letting out another meow.

"Yes, I know," she added, rolling her eyes, "you think I'm wasting my time. And don't worry, I won't be going to London again, not if I can help it. There's nothing there for me but -"

Before she could finish, she heard a gentle knock on the front door. Startled, she turned and looked through toward the hallway. She was so unaccustomed to visitors that her first thought was that she must be mistaken, but on some deeper level she could already sense a solitary heart beating very fast indeed on the door's other side. She glanced at Smythe, and then she walked through to the hallway, where she realized that the beating heart seemed a little small, as if it belong to a child.

Smythe meowed.

"I know," Lydia whispered, "but I can't just ignore it. It might be..."

She hesitated, before stepping forward and opening the door. To her surprise, she saw Verity Cain standing alone on the other side.

"I don't think you should be here," Lydia said cautiously. "Your parents -"

"Is it true?" Verity asked.

"Is what true?"

"I heard Mother and Father talking this morning," Verity continued, "and they said everyone around these parts knows that you're a -"

She paused, as if she was scared to say the final word.

"Witch," she managed finally.

"That's not necessarily how I'd describe it," Lydia said cautiously, before glancing around in case the other children might be nearby. "Listen, I meant what I told you just now. You shouldn't be here and I'm sure you'll get into a lot of trouble if your parents find out that you came. Where do they think you are right now, anyway? Don't they bother to check on you at all?"

"Do you know magic?" Verity asked.

"I really don't see the purpose of this conversation."

"Can you show me?" Verity continued. "Your magic, I mean. I don't know whether I believe in it, so I want to see it for myself so that I can make up my own mind."

"That's very wise of you," Lydia replied, "but I really have nothing to show you."

"So you're *not* a witch?"

Lydia opened her mouth to reply, but for a few seconds she held back. She hated the idea of lying, especially to such a young girl, but at the same time she knew that admitting the truth would amount to opening a whole different kettle of fish. She looked around again, and then she told herself that since 'witch' was a somewhat debatable term, she supposed that it couldn't necessarily be used to describe her own rather unique situation.

"No," she said finally, fudging the truth rather than outright lying, at least in her own mind, "I'm not a witch."

"Are you sure?"

"As sure as one can be," she continued. "You really need to stop listening to gossip, and remember that people can get awfully excited sometimes." Crouching down, she made sure to look properly into the girl's eyes, hoping to drive her point home a little more forcefully. "There are enough scary things in the world, Verity, without inventing even more. Trust me, you're so young right now and I suppose you don't really understand how life works. You should be enjoying your innocence while you can."

"So they're all lying?"

"Not lying, exactly, more... I suppose they're getting excited about things that simply aren't ever going to happen. And some of them are a little suspicious of a woman living all alone with just her cat for company."

"Why?"

"They just are," she said, realizing now that she wasn't likely to get through to the girl. Standing up again, she stepped forward and pulled the front door shut. "Come on, let me walk you to the road."

***

A couple of minutes later, making her way past the hedge and reaching the roadside, Lydia looked out across the glorious view of the Kentish countryside in winter.

"Will you be alright walking home by yourself?" she asked, turning to look back down at Verity. "It's just that I'm really not sure it'd be a good idea for you to be seen with me again. People might come up with all sorts of strange ideas. Even stranger than before."

"That's fine," Verity said, sounding a little more confident now. "Ms. Smith, I know everyone says very mean and horrible things about you, but I actually don't think you're as bad as they make you seem. I think I'm sorry for throwing things at your window and for calling you a witch."

"That's very kind of you," Lydia replied, "and I absolutely accept your apology most graciously."

"But if you ever *do* become a witch," Verity added, lowering her voice a little as if for some reason she was worried about being overheard, "would you mind terribly letting me know, and then teaching me some of your tricks? It all just sounds like so much fun, and I don't understand why anyone would be angry about it. After all, what's wrong with being able to do magical things?"

"I really don't know," Lydia said, wishing for a moment that she could grant the girl's wishes. "Now run along and get home safely, and I think it's best if you don't come to see me again. I'm sorry, but that's just the way things have to be."

"Alright," Verity said. She hesitated, clearly lost in thought, before suddenly stepping forward and putting her arms around Lydia for a big hug. "Thank you."

"For what?" Lydia asked, shocked by the human contact but realizing after a moment that this hug wasn't too upsetting after all.

"For not boiling me in a pot," Verity replied, hugging her a little tighter before letting go and stepping back, "or turning me into a frog, or doing any of the other horrible things that I heard witches can do."

"Even if I could do those things," Lydia

said, unable to stifle a faint smile, "I wouldn't."

Verity paused, as if she was on the verge of saying something else, and then she turned and hurried away along the road. Once she reached the far corner, she stopped for a moment and looked back at Lydia, before setting off again and racing into the distance. Lydia, meanwhile, watched as the girl disappeared from view, and she felt as if for once she'd actually managed to handle a situation rather well. There was no good that could possibly come from telling Verity the truth, and – as she briefly spotted the girl in the distance, running past a gate at the side of a field – she could only hope that the child would go on to have a long and very happy life.

Hearing another meow, she turned to see that Smythe had wandered out and was watching her from the top of the steps.

"Yes, I know," she said as she started to make her way back to the house, "you're probably hungry, aren't you? I'm sure I can find something nice for you to eat, something that makes a change from your usual diet of mice and rats." As she passed Smythe, she patted the top of his head before walking toward the front door. "I must see what I can find."

Left alone, Smythe looked out toward the road. His gaze was focused on the fields, and he knew that the village lay a little further off. After a few seconds his pupils dilated and his whiskers twitched, almost as if he knew that something bad was on its way.

CHAPTER EIGHT

BY THE TIME NIGHT had fallen and midnight was rolling around, Lydia had spent almost ten full hours working with her books. A solitary candle was burning on the desk, but even this was starting to burn down and the light had begun to flicker. Having told herself for a while now that she would stop for the night once the candle was done, Lydia had to accept now that this moment was almost at hand.

"Fascinating," she whispered as she finished another paragraph in one of the books. "It's all starting to come together now and -"

Hearing a creaking sound from above, she looked up at the ceiling. The flickering candle cast a dancing glow against one side of her face and picked out a hint of fear in her eyes. A faint scar was still just about visible on one of her cheeks. She watched the boards above, while listening keenly in case the sound returned, but after a few more seconds she allowed herself to relax just a little.

"Not now," she said softly. "It's too soon."

A strong wind blew outside, rattling the windows in their frames as she finally got to her feet. Stiff from having sat for so long, she made her way through to the hallway and into the kitchen, where she stopped to fill herself a glass of water. She was still thinking about all the discoveries she'd made during her latest round of research, and she had to admit that at times she wished she had someone – anyone – with whom she could discuss all her findings. At the same time, she knew that women in her position tended to live lonely lives, with only their familiars for company. A moment later she heard another creaking sound coming from upstairs, and she instinctively turned and looked at the staircase.

"Not now," she said again, a little more firmly this time. "I'm working hard, I promise. I almost -"

Suddenly she heard a heavy bang coming from the living room. Shocked, she froze for a moment before rushing back through, and she was surprised to see the back door swinging open. The door hit the wall, causing another bang, and Lydia quickly made her way over and pushed it shut before turning the key. She was sure that the door had previously been closed properly, but as she peered though the glass and saw nothing outside she had to acknowledge that the wind was really picking up out there.

"Everything's quite alright," she said under her breath, trying to calm her raging nerves.

Still, she remained at the door for a full minute, still looking out at the garden. She could hear the wind raging and the trees blowing nearby, but after a few seconds she realized that she was picking up on something else; she could sense several hearts beating in the vicinity, and these hearts were pounding harder and faster than anything she'd known before. These weren't children, she knew that now, and she tried to work out exactly where they might be lurking before – finally – she felt the hairs standing up on the back of her neck as she realized that the hearts were apparently beating *inside* the house.

She very slowly turned and looked across the living room. She saw no sign of anyone, but deep down she already knew with absolute certainty that she wasn't alone. Her eyes darted from one door to the next, and she realized after a few seconds that she was holding her breath as she listened out for any hint of movement.

She swallowed hard.

Suddenly she heard a cry, followed by the

sound of Smythe screaming, and she watched as a man stumbled into the living room with the cat attached to his face. Horrified, Lydia could only watch as the man fell back over a chair and landed hard on the ground with Smythe still clinging to his features and biting down hard on his cheek.

"Smythe!" she called out, rushing over. "Leave him alone! Don't -"

Before she could finish, she sensed more movement nearby. She turned just in time to see two other men rushing through from the kitchen. Filled with a sudden sense of panic, she reached a hand out toward them; in that instant, a nearby table flipped over and flew through the air, smashing into both men with such force that they immediately fell down. A fraction of a second later, three more men rushed through, but they stopped when they realized what had befallen their comrades and Lydia immediately saw the terror in their eyes.

At that moment, she felt fury coursing through her body.

"What are you doing in my home?" she snarled, clenching her fists. "Have you come here to kill me?"

"Witch!" one of the men shouted, holding up a crucifix. "Be gone, you fearful -"

Without even meaning to do so, Lydia tilted her head, ripping the crucifix from the man's hand and sending it slamming into the wall so hard that it became embedded in the plaster.

"This is *my* home," she said breathlessly, as Smythe continued to bite at the face of the man on the ground, who seemed powerless to push him away, "and I will not tolerate any intrusion."

She saw more men stepping into view from the hallway, and she realized that while one or two had initially made their way inside through the back door, they must have then opened the door at the front to let the rest enter.

"So what was your plan, exactly?" she continued, unable to disguise a sense of genuine disgust. "Were you simply going to cut my throat? Were you going to burn me? Or were you thinking of something a little more old-fashioned? Someone had me on a ducking stool once, and that didn't work out too well for him. I'm afraid that if you want to get the better of me, you need to be a whole lot quicker than this."

She looked at each man in turn, waiting to see if one of them would make the potentially fatal mistake of lunging at her. Although she hated the idea of causing pain, in that moment she knew that her only option would be lethal force, and she supposed that she'd just have to deal with the consequences later.

"Well?" she called out, frustrated by their gormless faces as they all simply stood there like fools. "Will one of you please say something? Are you going to try to finish the job or not?"

***

"They're gone," she whispered a short while later, standing at the front door and watching as the men disappeared around the corner, heading off into the night with their tails very much between their legs. "At least for now."

Feeling utterly exhausted, she sat down in the doorway just as Smythe made his way over. As he purred and brushed against her arm, she looked down and saw some blood around his jaw.

"That suits you, in a strange kind of way," she admitted as she gently stroked his side. "Not that I condone your use of violence, of course." She paused, gaining some degree of comfort from his presence. "I always said that if trouble arrived here at Styre House, we'd leave. I know I made that promise to you, Smythe, but you have to understand that things have changed. How can we leave now when..."

Her voice trailed off, and after a moment she turned and looked back into the house. She watched the staircase for a moment, and she felt a rush of relief as she realized that at least none of the intruders had gone up there. For a few seconds she tried to work out what would have happened if even one of them had gone into the spare bedroom, and a shiver ran through her bones as she imagined the sheer horror of what would inevitably have happened next. After more than a decade of keeping her greatest secret, she simply couldn't even begin to comprehend what might have occurred if one or more of those men had found...

Smythe let out a quiet meow.

"No, they're definitely gone for tonight," she continued. "I can sense that. There was a moment when they might have mounted more of a fight, but that passed quickly enough and they slunk off into the night like the pathetic non-entities that they are. They might very well come back later, and I'll need to be ready for that, but at least tonight we're safe."

Another meow.

"I wish I could *really* understand what you're trying to say," she told him. "I bet you'd have so many useful insights into everything that's going on. Of course, you'd probably also be busy telling me that I'm the most terrible old fool. Or young fool. I'm not even sure that I know the difference these days."

She stroked the side of his face.

"You don't seem to age either, do you?" she pointed out. "Like me. I suppose we're just... two peas in a pod, thrown together by a strange twist of fate ever since my father first found you on the side of the road. Or do you believe in destiny? Do you think that, in some way, we were always going to end up like this?"

Smythe meowed yet again.

"Oh, you're really no help at all, are you?" she laughed, but the laugh faded as she looked out at the night again. "I'll tell you one thing, though, Smythe. Those men won't simply give up. Not for long. Their first visit went very badly wrong for them, but they'll learn and now I'm certain that they'll be back. That can only mean one thing." She paused for a few seconds. "I'm running out of time. I have to work harder and faster than ever before."

CHAPTER NINE

ANOTHER CANDLE FLICKERED ON the floor in the middle of the room, as Lydia sat cross-legged with one of her notebooks opened nearby. She'd been reading the same passage over and over, trying to drill the words into her mind more clearly than ever before, but she knew that the right moment had almost arrived.

All that held her back now was fear.

"It's time," she whispered, before glancing over at Smythe as he watched her from the safe vantage point of a nearby chair. "I've been putting this off for so long. I just hope... I mean, I hope there won't be too much pain. Not for me, you understand, but for..."

Her voice trailed off for a few seconds, and then she looked up at the ceiling. She heard no telltale creaking sound, not this time, but the silence failed to lift her spirits.

"I'm going to do my best," she said firmly as tears began to fill her eyes. "That's what I promised all those years ago, and it's all I can do now. My *very* best."

She slowly looked down at the notebook again.

"Shadows come and shadows go," she read out loud, "and reach through worlds to promise me."

She paused, worried about what might happen once she finished reading this particular section.

"So show me now, as I demand," she added, closing her eyes as her voice trembled with fear. "Show me now what sure must be."

She waited, but so far she felt no change at all. She'd been hoping for a while now that this particular passage might help her to understand the next step, yet the whole thing was starting to feel like an anticlimax.

All she felt now was -

"Oh Parker, can you please stop complaining?" a woman's voice said suddenly, ringing out loud and clear in the room. "You've done nothing but moan since we got here. Can't you at least try to be constructive? You have no idea how exhausting you can be with all this endless negativity!"

As Lydia opened her eyes, something brushed against her. Shocked, she pulled back and turned; she saw no sign of anyone, but for a few seconds she heard footsteps heading out of the room and rushing through into the kitchen. Scrambling to her feet, she turned to follow, but when she reached the doorway she saw that the kitchen was entirely empty.

"I just don't see how this place is ever going to amount to anything," another female voice called out from one of the other rooms. "This entire project is a complete dead end. The sooner you realize that, the sooner we can go home!"

"We are home!" the first voice said firmly.

Turning to look the other way, Lydia tried to work out exactly how these two voices were reaching through to her. Although her first thought was that they might be voices from the past, she couldn't help but notice that there was something rather rough and uncouth about them, and on some deep level she began to suspect that they might actually come from somewhere else entirely.

The future.

"Hello?" she called out, even though she knew full well that she couldn't sense any heartbeats nearby. "Is someone here?"

She waited.

Silence.

"Parker?" she continued, although she wasn't even sure that Parker could possibly be a name at all. Indeed, as a name, Parker seemed utterly impossible and rather odd. "Either I'm losing my mind or..."

She considered the possibilities, but after a moment she realized that there was really only one obvious likelihood. Was it possible that the 'spell' (a word she hated) had worked slightly differently to how she'd expected, and that instead of divining the future she'd actually briefly been able to witness something that would one day happen in the house? Confused by the thought of future events somehow existing in what she considered to be the present day, she made her way back into the living room and looked down at the notebooks. A moment later she glanced over at Smythe and saw that he still hadn't moved from the chair.

"Every time I think I understand how this works," she told him, "I quickly find that there's so much more to learn. Smythe... what if I truly just saw into the future?"

***

Eight hours later, with sunlight rising outside and spreading into the house, Lydia took a deep breath and prepared to speak the words for what felt like the ten millionth time.

"Shadows come and shadows go," she said calmly, "and reach through worlds to promise me. So show me now, as I demand. Show me now what sure must be."

She waited, as she had waited so many times before, yet once again she saw and heard nothing. The very first time she'd tried the words, she'd heard the voices of two women speaking to each other, yet every time since she'd had no luck at all. Now, with morning having arrived after a sleepless night, she was starting to feel as if she'd completely wasted her time. Leaning back against the side of the chair, she briefly considered trying again, before finally accepting that for some reason her luck had truly run out.

"Stupid powers!" she hissed, kicking the notebooks away as she was briefly overwhelmed by a sense of frustration. "How much more would I be able to do if I *really* understood them properly?"

Feeling utterly foolish, she simply sat on the floor for a moment before realizing that Smythe – who'd been drifting in and out of sleep on the chair all night – was watching her again.

"Don't give me that look!" she snapped. "Sorry, I didn't mean to take it out on you, Smythe, it's just that I feel I take two steps back for every stumbling lurch forward. Obviously I achieved something when I read those words for the first time, but now it's as if I'm just rambling pointlessly.

I don't suppose you have any insights, do you?"

Smythe flicked his tail slightly, but otherwise he offered no response and genuinely seemed entirely untroubled by the situation.

"And now I've wasted another night," Lydia said with yet another sigh. "I'm acting like I have all the time in the world, when I don't. Or, rather, she..."

Her voice trailed off as she felt a shudder pass through the marrow of her bones.

"I made a promise," she added, "and I swore all those years ago that I'd find a way to keep that promise."

Getting to her feet, she rubbed her eyes and told herself that she absolutely couldn't afford to sleep. She was already thinking of all the things she needed to pick up from the village, and she quickly resolved to head out and get a few chores done. Making her way to the kitchen, she pulled some bread out and began to tear it into chunks, making sure to set aside enough for two people.

Once she was done with that, she spent the next hour or so working on various jobs around the house, before slipping her feet into her shoes and walking quickly to the front door.

"I won't be too long, Smythe," she called out wearily. "It's just best to get these jobs done now, as soon as the shops in the village open, so that I can come back and devote the whole day to some more study. I'm sure you'll be fine for a while."

As soon as she was outside, she took care to lock the door properly. Every bone in her body was tired and she simply wanted to sleep, but at the same time she was driven by an overwhelming determination to fulfill her promise; for that to happen, she realized, she needed to use her time as wisely as possible, so as she hurried down the steps she was already making a mental note to fetch enough items to last for a few days. She hated going to the village at the best of times, since she knew that she was loathed by everyone there, but she supposed that the men from the previous night would be too busy licking their wounds to try anything in broad daylight. They might, she reasoned, be back after nightfall, but she told herself to focus on one problem at a time.

As she hurried away from the house, she failed to notice that she was being watched by a figure who'd been hiding behind a nearby tree. And as she made her way toward the end of the road, she also failed to look over her shoulder; had she done so, she would have seen the figure darting out from behind the tree and hurrying up the steps that led to Styre House.

AMY CROSS

CHAPTER TEN

THE KNIFE'S THIN BLADE slid into the lock and jiggled around for a moment, before a heavy clunking sound indicated success. A hand gripped the handle and gave it a turn, pulling the door open, and then Jimmy Ward stopped and looked over his shoulder.

Several minutes had passed since he'd seen Lydia Smith hurrying off toward the village. Jimmy calculated that, unless she turned back for some unforeseen reason, he had at least an hour and a half to look around the house, and he supposed that the task wouldn't take that long at all. He waited for a moment longer, before pulling the knife out of the lock and slipping into the house, and then bumping the door shut gently.

Hearing a shuffling sound, he turned just in

time to see a black cat stepping into view.

"Puss, hey," Jimmy said softly. "Don't worry, I'm not here to cause any trouble. I'm a... friend... well, an acquaintance really of your owner. I've met Ms. Smith once and..."

He tried to think of a way to finish that sentence that wouldn't be a complete lie.

"I just popped down to check on a few things," he added, feeling a little uncomfortable as he realized that the cat was glaring at him with a strangely determined – almost judgmental – expression. "Relax, I'm not going to take anything and I won't cause any trouble. I came all the way down here from London, just to prove to myself that my suspicions are wrong." He looked around the hallway for a moment. "They *have* to be wrong. Lydia Smith can't be in her eighties."

Making his way toward one of the open doorways, he reached down to stroke the cat.

"I don't suppose you know anything about that, do you?" he asked. "What kind of -"

In that moment, Smythe hissed loudly and swiped at Jimmy's hand with his claws. Wincing, Jimmy pulled back and saw scratches around his wrist.

"Alright," he muttered, "that's fair enough. After all, this is your home too and I'm an intruder. Just don't tell anyone that I was ever here. There's really no need for Ms. Smith to ever find out."

Heading into the front room, he saw a pile of notebooks on the table. He wandered over and ran a hand along the table's smooth surface.

"Good quality," he said, raising both eyebrows. "She clearly knows a little about decent furniture."

He opened one of the notebooks, and he was immediately fascinated by the scrawled text he found inside.

"Well," he continued, taking a seat as he told himself that he had time to at least peruse a few of the pages, "it would seem that Ms. Smith is quite the scholar. Even more than I'd realized." He turned to another page. "The question is, though... a scholar of *what*, precisely?"

***

Around one hour later, still sitting at the desk and looking through notebook after notebook, Jimmy wasn't much closer to finding an answer to his question.

"This is clearly some very sophisticated work," he mused out loud, assuming that the cat was probably listening. "She obviously knows what she's going on about, even if she's made no attempt to clarify any of it for a reader. Then again, I suppose she never intended for anyone else to see it."

He glanced to his left and saw Smythe sitting in the doorway, glaring at him with an expression of unmistakable loathing.

"Oh, don't look at me like that," he continued. "I'm going to put everything back how I found it." He glanced at the clock on the mantelpiece, and in that moment he closed the notebook. "Which I should be doing round about now, actually," he added, before getting to his feet. "Your mistress will be back soon and I absolutely mustn't be caught snooping around. I really wouldn't know where to begin defending my actions. Frankly, she'd have every right to call the police on me."

Once he'd made sure that everything on the desk was back to how he'd found it, Jimmy hurried to the window and looked out at the garden. He waited for a moment, watching for any hint that Lydia might be on her way back already, and then he slipped through to the hallway. He hadn't even been quite sure what he was expecting, but so far all he'd discovered was that Lydia was into some pretty unusual research topics, although he knew that was no crime. Approaching the front door, he reached for the handle, but at the last second he stopped as he heard a floorboard creaking somewhere upstairs.

Slowly he turned and looked over his shoulder. The staircase seemed bare and innocent, and until that moment he'd assumed that his only company in the house was that pesky black cat.

Now, however, he felt a cold sweat running across his features as he realized that there seemed to be something – or someone – up in one of the bedrooms.

Hearing a meowing sound, he turned and saw that the cat had followed him through to the hallway. Something about the creature's eyes seemed so calm and knowing now, and Jimmy couldn't shake the feeling that he was being watched very intently.

"Is there someone else here?" he mouthed silently.

He stood completely still for a couple of minutes, but he heard no further sign of movement and he began to hope that he might have been mistaken. Still, he figured that Lydia wasn't supposed to get home for a while yet, and after a moment – slightly against his better judgment but driven by innate curiosity – he walked over to the bottom of the stairs and looked up toward the landing.

Again he waited.

Again, he heard only silence – at least until the cat meowed again.

"Alright, I get it," he said. "I told you already, I'm not going to cause trouble. I just want to..."

He looked up the staircase again.

"... make sure..."

After a moment's further consideration, he began to walk up to the landing. The cat quickly hurried past, running to the top and then stopping to look back down at him, and Jimmy couldn't help but notice that the creature seemed a little more troubled by something now. Sure enough, when he got to the top himself, Jimmy watched as the cat rushed over to a nearby closed door and sat down, almost as if it was trying to guard that particular room.

"What's got your fur all ruffled suddenly?" Jimmy asked.

He stepped toward the door, but Smythe immediately hissed, baring his fangs in what was clearly some kind of warning.

"You're not happy now, are you?" Jimmy continued. "What -"

In that instant, he heard a faint bumping sound coming from the other side of the door.

"There's someone here," he whispered, worried now that his cover had been blown wide open. He paused, but he knew that he had to defuse the situation as rapidly as possible. "Hello?" he called out. "I'm terribly sorry, but there's been some kind of mistake and I'm just going to leave now. Please, I don't mean to hurt or -"

Before he could finish, he heard a faint gasping sound coming from inside the room. He hesitated, listening as the sound continued, but he was starting to think that the person in the room might need help. Torn between the desire to get as far away as possible and an unflinching duty to help someone who might be in distress, he paused for a moment longer before stepping closer to the door. As soon as he reached for the handle, however, Smythe let out a much louder and much angrier snarl.

"Easy there," Jimmy said, "I only -"

Before he could finish, Smythe swiped at him with exposed claws. Shocked, Jimmy took a step back, and he was starting to worry whether the cat was ever going to let him open the door.

"What's in there?" he asked. "Who is it?"

Hearing the gasping sound once more, Jimmy could tell now with absolute certainty that someone was in trouble. He reached for the handle again, and again the cat hissed a warning. And then, just as Jimmy was having to decide whether to force his way past, Smythe fell silent and rushed past him, hurrying to the stairs.

"That's better," Jimmy muttered, taking a moment to adjust his collar before grabbing the handle and pushing the door open gently. "Hello?" he called out. "I'm truly sorry, I don't mean to intrude but -"

And then he saw her. A woman was on the bed, wrapped in filthy sheets; emaciated and clearly ill, with a shock of unruly hair, she glared back at him with milky white eyes. She opened her mouth and let out an angry snarl, in the process exposing two rows of blackened, rotten teeth.

"Who are you?" Jimmy stammered.

"You shouldn't be here," a voice said firmly.

Turning, Jimmy saw that Lydia was reaching the top of the staircase, with Smythe following.

"Who's that woman?" Jimmy asked.

"You've made a terrible mistake," Lydia sneered, before taking a step forward and looking past him, watching as the woman on the bed pulled against chains that kept her bound tight to the headboard. "That woman is Rebecca Barnett, and she's here because I have to put right something that once went so utterly, terribly wrong."

CHAPTER ELEVEN

"SHE DOESN'T STIR OFTEN," Lydia explained as she and Jimmy sat at the dining room downstairs. Picking at her fingernails, Lydia was clearly deeply uncomfortable. "I think that's probably for the best. Most of the time, she's in this almost fugue-like state, almost as if she's barely awake."

"I still don't understand what she's doing here," he replied sternly. "That woman needs urgent medical attention."

"She's far beyond the reach of conventional medicine," Lydia told him.

"A doctor -"

"A doctor would take one look at her," she continued, "and throw her into the deepest, darkest cell in an asylum. He'd conclude that there's nothing that can be done to help her, and he might well be right but... I have to try."

"Try *what*, exactly?"

He waited for an answer, and then he looked over at the notebooks.

"There's an answer in there somewhere," Lydia said, struggling once again to hold back tears. "I know there is. There has to be. One thing I've learned is that these powers are very... balanced. So if they made her like this, then they have to be able to undo that damage."

"Are you seriously trying to tell me that something in some dusty old books made her like that?"

"When she first came here a little over a decade ago," Lydia replied, "she was a vibrant and healthy young woman with a very keen intellect. I was in awe of her, actually, at least in some ways. Her problem, however, was that she didn't know when to stop. She just wanted to learn more and more, and I couldn't hold her back. She first came to my door because she'd heard that I had a lot of books, and she wanted to read as much as she could. She didn't even care what they were about, she just wanted knowledge. Reading between the lines, I think she was frustrated by her little life in the village."

"So you... taught her?"

"No, absolutely not," Lydia said, shaking her head firmly before pausing for a moment. "At least, not in the way you're thinking. She was persistent. I hadn't been here at Styre House for that long, and I suppose I felt a little lonely so I let my defenses down. I'll never forgive myself for that. But I decided that if I hid away my notebooks about... the darker arts... then I could use what was left to teach her some safe knowledge. About plants and animals, that sort of thing. Nothing a well-educated young man wouldn't pick up at one of our nation's finest universities."

"Then what went wrong?" he asked, still looking at the notebooks.

"Why are you here, Mr. Ward?"

"I'm here because -"

"I was halfway to the village when I sensed you. Did you really think that you could just walk into my home without getting caught?"

"Sensed me?" He paused. "What exactly do you mean by that?"

"You're here because you noticed a discrepancy in the details I supplied when I joined the library," she said, interrupting him. "Yes, you rather blabbed that out when you panicked just now and tried to excuse your intrusion into my home. But a mere discrepancy isn't enough to bring you all the way down here from London, is it? I can't help thinking that the *real* reason you're here is that you couldn't simply put that discrepancy down to a mistake."

He opened his mouth to reply, but instead he held back.

"I might have been using a relative's membership," she pointed out. "A mother, perhaps, or an aunt. Or a cleric might simply have written down the wrong year. There were several possible explanations, but you seem to have jumped to the more surreal idea that I'm somehow much, much older than I appear. In turn, that suggests to me that you have an unusual openness to such concepts."

"I've studied local legends in great depth," he said cautiously. "I put together just enough facts to... I suppose you could say that my curiosity was piqued."

"Enough to break into my home?"

"I have already apologized and -"

"Relax, Mr. Ward," she added, cutting him off yet again. "I'm not going to admonish you for your actions. Far from it. The truth is, I respect your curiosity. But when I tell you what really happened to poor Rebecca, I'm afraid you might wish you'd never left your desk in London."

***

1889, twelve years earlier...

"That's another very interesting herb," Lydia said, as she slid the next book across the table. "It's a type of nettle, but most people would never guess that fact. It can actually be used for the treatment of a variety of skin conditions. Do you remember the name of the other herb we discussed last week that can also be used in that way?"

She waited for an answer, but Rebecca – while most certainly looking at the book – seemed to be off in a world of her own.

"Rebecca?"

"Hmm?"

Looking up, Rebecca appeared rather startled now.

"I don't think," Lydia continued, "that lessons about herbs are really grabbing your attention." She closed the book. "Is there some other subject you'd rather study?"

"I didn't mean to be rude, Lydia," Rebecca replied cautiously. "Please, you must never think that. It's just that I've learned an awful lot in these lessons with you, but I know..."

She paused, before turning and looking at the cabinet on the far side of the room.

"Perhaps," Lydia said after a moment, "our little lessons have reached a natural end."

"I just know that there's other knowledge here," Rebecca explained after a moment, with a faraway tone to her voice. "I've heard whispers in the village. Rumors, really. Nothing more than gossip. Some people say that you know more than most people."

"You shouldn't listen to such talk," Lydia replied.

"But is it true?"

At this, Lydia could only sigh.

"I'm talking about forbidden knowledge," Rebecca continued, and now she seemed far more excited than at any point during the actual lesson. "Please, Lydia, do me the honor of not lying to me about it again. I've seen with my own eyes the way you react if I go anywhere near that cabinet, and I know you keep it locked at all times. I know you keep the key on a chain around your neck, too."

Reaching up, Lydia instinctively touched the necklace. Until that moment, she hadn't realized that Rebecca had noticed it at all.

"I saw you use it to open the cabinet once," Rebecca said nervously, "when you thought I wasn't watching, and there are notebooks in there. What kind of notebooks do you have, what could they possibly contain, that makes you so scared to let them out?"

"Rebecca..."

"I'm ready," she added, with a hint of desperation in her voice. "Please, can't you at least let me try?"

"It's complicated."

"If you can handle it, then why can't I?"

"Because I can *barely* handle it," Lydia

countered. "Believe me, the struggle is constant. There are times when I feel that I'm on the verge of completely losing control, and I have to force myself to step back." Getting to her feet, she saw Smythe watching from a nearby chair. "I knew I was wrong to start giving you these lessons. You begged and begged, and eventually I thought that you'd be satisfied, but now I see that's never going to be the case." She turned to Rebecca again. "Please don't be upset, but today is our last meeting."

"No!" Rebecca gasped. "Please, forget I said anything."

She grabbed one of the books and pulled it closer, opening it at a page filled with drawings of local wild flowers.

"Where was the part about the nettles again?" she asked, frantically flicking through the book. "That's what you were going on about, isn't it? See, I do listen!"

"Rebecca -"

"I can't go back to how I was before," Rebecca said firmly, looking up at her. "Please, Lydia, I'm sorry I pressed you to tell me about those other books, I'll never do anything like that ever again. I just want to know more about the world, and if that means reading about nettles and dandelions and such things, then I shan't ever complain again." She waited for an answer.

"Please?"

Lydia truly wanted to end the lessons there and then, but after a moment's consideration she sat back down. Although she still felt as if she was making a truly dreadful mistake, she hated the idea of cutting Rebecca loose and she told herself that she could give the girl one last chance. After all, what harm could there possibly be in offering someone some kind of basic education? She'd been in Rebecca's shoes once, bored and isolated and frustrated, and she truly wanted to help.

"Please?" Rebecca said yet again.

"I was telling you about a type of nettle that can be used to treat skin conditions," Lydia said cautiously, still unable to quite shake the sense that she was making a terrible error of judgment. She paused, she swallowed, and then she resolved to keep going. "Some of these nettles can be really rather fascinating. They grow by the side of the road and people go past without even glancing at them, yet some of them hold the most remarkable restorative powers."

"How interesting," Rebecca said, beaming from ear to ear. "Please, Lydia... tell me more!"

CHAPTER TWELVE

A FEW DAYS LATER, as she made her way along the street in the middle of the village, Lydia couldn't help but notice that once again several of the locals were casting suspicious looks her way. That much was fairly usual, but on this occasion she was noticing even more of a frosty atmosphere. By the time she entered the village shop, she couldn't help but wonder whether something else might be wrong.

"Good morning, Ms. Smith," the woman behind the counter said somewhat archly. "Will it be your usual order today?"

"Please," Lydia replied, stopping and watching as the woman set to work gathering up various items. "It's rather pleasant out there," she added, supposing that she should try to get some small-talk going even though she usually loathed such things. "I rather think that we might finally be done with that spell of rainy weather."

She waited for an answer, but on this occasion the shopkeeper – who was usually perfectly polite – said nothing.

"I suppose the farmers will be pleased," she continued, forcing a smile. "They'll be able to start making plans for their harvests now."

Again she waited, but as the woman made her way back over Lydia couldn't help but notice a distinctly uncomfortable expression on her face.

"I hear," the shopkeeper murmured finally as she began to wrap Lydia's items, "that you've been teaching the Barnett girl."

"Where did you hear that?" Lydia asked, bristling slightly. Ever since starting to teach Rebecca, she'd sworn the girl to secrecy about their little arrangement.

"Oh, word spreads. People have seen her heading out your way, and there's not much else in that direction, is there?"

"I'm sure I don't know *what* she gets up to," Lydia replied.

"So it's not true?"

"I have met her a few times," Lydia explained, trying to skate around the truth somewhat, "but you know what young women are like. I'm sure she just goes out exploring."

"That's possible, I suppose," the woman muttered.

"I know that if I'd grown up around here," Lydia continued, "I'd have been out there in the countryside all the time. Nobody would have been able to stop me venturing forth whenever I had the chance. I've always been very good at spending time on my own, and it's possible that young Rebecca simply feels the same way."

"Let's hope you're right," the shopkeeper replied, offering her a worried glance before looking back down at the package she was still assembling. "A lot of people around these parts don't like it when girls get too curious. They think it's a bad sign. If you ask me, Rebecca would do better to stay at home more and learn from her own mother. That's how things usually work."

***

As she reached the steps that led up to the front door, Lydia was surprised to see Smythe sitting at the top as if he was waiting for her.

"You're alert this morning," she said as she made her way up to join him. She reached down to pat the top of his head, but he immediately turned and darted toward the door before stopping and looking back, clearly checking to make sure that she was following.

Lydia furrowed her brow.

"Whatever has gotten into you?" she asked, carrying her bag of items across the garden, only for Smythe to turn and start pawing at the door. "Smythe, you're worrying me a little. Shouldn't you be off catching vermin somewhere in the garden?"

She opened the door, and Smythe immediately bolted toward the living room, only to stop suddenly as if he'd seen something around the corner.

"I shall never quite understand what goes on in that little head of yours," Lydia admitted. "Sometimes I wish that I could -"

In that moment, she heard a rustling sound, followed by a faint bump and then a gasp.

"Who's there?" she asked, setting the bag down and hurrying to the doorway. "What -"

Stopping suddenly, she saw to her horror that Rebecca was kneeling on the floor, surrounded by notebooks. After glancing at the cabinet and seeing that it was somehow open, Lydia rushed around and dropped to her knees in front of Rebecca, who was muttering under her breath while running a fingertip across some of the scrawled text.

"What are you doing here?" Lydia asked, trying to grab the notebook, only for Rebecca to push her away. "You're not supposed to come back until Monday!"

"Tell me how to fix it!" Rebecca hissed, her

voice sounding deep and scratched.

"How did you get into that cabinet?" Lydia stammered, double-checking that the key was still hanging around her neck.

"I managed to break through the back section," Rebecca explained, frantically turning to the next page. "Lydia, please don't be angry with me, but I just wanted to learn a little of what's in here. I think I might have made a small mistake, though. I've been reading some of it out loud, and each time sometimes seems to... change in me. And now I can't undo it, and every time I try to make things better I just end up making it so much worse."

"You fool!" Lydia snapped angrily. "You have to stop this before it's too late! How long have you been here?"

"Help me!" Rebecca replied. "I can fix this."

"No, you really can't," Lydia insisted, trying again to take the notebook from her. "You just have to stop before you get in too far, because otherwise -"

"Go away!" Rebecca roared, looking up at her for the first time, revealing jet black eyes that were already leaking a strange grayish liquid down her face. "If you can't help, then at least stop distracting me!"

Horrified by the sight of the girl's face,

Lydia could only stare for a moment before suddenly Rebecca pushed her back. As she fell against the side of the chair, Lydia saw Rebecca already returning her attention to the book and muttering loudly as if she truly believed that she could simply find some easy way to undo all the mistakes she'd already made. Frozen by a mounting sense of fear, Lydia felt for a moment as if there was simply no way she could set everything right.

"I'm nearly there," Rebecca groaned, turning the pages with hands that looked strangely pale. "I thought I could just dabble a bit. I didn't realize that once I started -"

"Rebecca, listen to me," Lydia said firmly, crawling back over to her as Smythe watched from the doorway. "This can all be fixed, but you're going to have to listen to me extremely carefully. Stop what you're doing at once and let me talk you through the only way to undo all the mistakes you've made so far." She waited for a reply, but Rebecca was still talking to herself and seemed not to have heard at all. "Rebecca? I want you to focus on my voice and let me lead you out of your current thoughts. Can you do that?"

"Shut up!" Rebecca snarled.

"You're digging yourself deeper and deeper into this mess," Lydia continued, "and soon you won't be able to ever get out again." Reaching out, she touched Rebecca's hand, and she was shocked to feel that the girl's flesh was so terribly icy. "You have to let me help you. It's the only way."

"You can help me by leaving me alone," Rebecca replied.

"That's really not how it works," Lydia said firmly. "I have experience with these things. Not much, and maybe not enough, but certainly more than you. Please, you have to listen to me and trust that I know how to undo it all, because otherwise you're liable to get lost forever in the darkness." She kept hold of the girl's hand, even though she still hated the sensation of touching another human being. "Are you listening to me, Rebecca? Please, just let me know that -"

"Shut up!" Rebecca screamed, suddenly launching herself at Lydia, slamming her against the ground before climbing on top of her and grabbing her by the throat. "Why are you making this so much harder? Why can't you leave me alone to get this right?"

"Stop!" Lydia gasped, trying to pull free as she felt Rebecca's grip tightening. "Please..."

"You want those books all to yourself!" Rebecca sneered, as the darkness in her eyes leaked down onto her face and blood began to dribble from one corner of her mouth. "That's the big problem here, isn't it? You want them all to yourself and you think you don't have to share with anyone! But that's not fair! You don't get to keep this knowledge and not share it! It doesn't belong to you, Lydia, and I won't let you control me! This power is mine now and I won't let anyone ever take it away from me!"

CHAPTER THIRTEEN

1901, twelve years later...

THE BEDROOM DOOR CREAKED open gently, allowing Lydia and Jimmy to look through at the horrific sight of Rebecca Barnett still chained to the bed.

"I managed to fight her off," Lydia explained, her voice tense with fear as she saw Rebecca's milky eyes glaring back at her. "Smythe helped a little with that."

"Smythe?"

Hearing a meowing sound, Jimmy turned and saw the black cat reaching the top of the staircase behind them.

"It was a miracle – I hate that word – but somehow I was able to subdue her, and then I got her up here and chained her to the bed. By that point she was screaming at me, telling me that I didn't understand and that she was going to make me burn. To be honest, for a while I wondered whether she might be able to do just that, but gradually I established that she had no real control over her new powers. She has been filled with chaos ever since, and although I long believed that I'd be able to cure her, the reality is..."

She hesitated, faced now with the full truth of her failure.

"Without knowing exactly what she read all those years ago," she continued, "I quickly found that I was only making things worse."

"What *exactly* is wrong with her?" Jimmy asked.

"Her mind is broken," Lydia said firmly. "Unfortunately, bad knowledge has seeped into the resulting cracks. I'm reasonably sure that her sanity is permanently gone and that nothing can be done for her, but I've spent more than a decade trying to prove myself wrong and come up with a solution. She used to be such a smart and clever young girl, with a bright future ahead of her. If there's even a small chance to save her, I can't give up."

"And you've had her chained up here for more than ten years?"

"For my sins, yes," she explained. "She sleeps a lot. I feed her twice a day, but apart from that she's very quiet and in truth I'm able to focus on my work. She has no way of escaping, of that I'm sure, and there are times when I very deliberately try to forget that she's even here. I search tirelessly through my notebooks, I research as much as I can, I devote my every waking moment to the task of trying to find a cure. Even if that cure isn't permanent, even if – as I have long suspected – she must die, I would at least like her to become more herself for her final moments. Is that too much to ask?"

"She must have family," he pointed out. "People must have come looking for her."

"And I dissuaded them from coming again," she replied. "They used to come marching right up to my door, demanding to know what I'd done with her, but I had a little knack of making them turn around and march right off again. It's imperfect, and I know a lot of people in the village have their suspicions. The illusion holds for now, although I know eventually they'll come for me again. They almost got me the other night. I just have to hope that before that happens, I can somehow save poor Rebecca's soul. She needs -"

"Give me the notebooks!" Rebecca snarled, pulling once again on the chains.

"She can talk," Jimmy whispered, resisting the urge to step back.

"Whore, give me those notebooks!"

Rebecca hissed, clearly becoming more and more agitated. "You don't know how to use them, but *I* do! It'll take me five minutes to free myself if you just let me read them!"

"She's deluded," Lydia whispered. "This is the dark side of the power. It can corrupt the mind so completely that all rational thought is gone. There's no -"

"Give me those notebooks, you bitch!" Rebecca screamed, pulling harder and harder on the chains now, causing the entire bed to rattle and shake.

"We're agitating her," Lydia said, stepping back and grabbing the handle.

"Why won't you just let me fix this?" Rebecca shouted. "Let me out of here you c-"

The door bumped shut. Lydia flinched, but already the voice on the other side of the door had become much more muted.

"When she can't see me, she's less angry," Lydia said softly. "She blames me for her predicament, and she's completely right to do so. I never should have even let her into my house. Now you see why I have a solemn duty to save her from this darkness."

"You can't blame yourself entirely," Jimmy replied, reaching out and putting a hand on the side of her arm. "Lydia -"

"Don't!" she snapped, recoiling from his

touch.

"I'm sorry."

"You're an intruder here and you don't understand," she continued, clearly on the verge of panic. "I don't need help, I can manage the situation perfectly well on my own. I'm already close to a breakthrough, I just need to focus on the final parts of the mystery and then I'm sure I can find a way to help her."

"I've studied such things," he replied. "Do you think I can help?"

She shook her head.

"Don't be so quick to dismiss my offer," he continued, watching her carefully. "I might know more than you think."

"You don't know anything."

"Not even about Old Mother Marston?" he added, and he immediately saw the change in her expression when she heard that name. "I know more than you might imagine, Lydia, and I won't tell anyone what's going on here. So where's the harm in at least letting me try to help?"

***

"You've made some astounding progress here," he said a short while later, as he looked at another of the notebooks in the front room downstairs. "I took a little peek earlier, but now that you've explained it to me, I'm starting to see some degree of sense emerging from the madness."

"I think most of the pieces of the puzzle are here," Lydia told him. "It's just a matter of putting them into the right order."

"But how do you know that Rebecca used a mix of these exact words?" he asked. "If she was experimenting, could she have tried making some up?"

"She could."

"Then -"

"But if that's the case," Lydia added, interrupting him, "then there's no hope whatsoever. I have to hope and pray that she didn't stray from the text in these notebooks."

"Do you have any of Old Mother Marston's books?"

"I'm afraid not," she replied. "They were all destroyed a long time ago. I've retained most of the information in them, though. Somehow the words seemed to become... burned into my mind."

"Useful," he suggested with a faint smile.

"And how do you know about Old Mother Marston?" she asked. "I thought she was completely forgotten."

"She crops up in a surprising number of cases in the local area," he explained, "dating back well over a century. She seems to have been some kind of... curator of literature relating to the supernatural. Actually, I've spent quite some time trying to dig into her story a little more. I'm certain that she's a fascinating figure, if I can just pinpoint a few more details about her." He paused. "Did you ever meet her?"

"No. I mean, not really."

"Not really?"

"I was at her home once," Lydia explained, "a short while after she died. I might have encountered her ghost."

"I'd like very much to know where that home was located."

"It was in -"

She caught herself just in time.

"I'm not sure that it's a good idea to go rooting around in such things," she continued. "I feel as if all this trouble started when my father took some books from her little cottage."

"I heard about her books," he admitted. "Some of them, according to legend, were even bound using leather made of... well, they say a few people went missing around that time."

"I don't claim to know everything about Old Mother Marston," Lydia replied, "and I'm not sure that I *want* to know. Right now, if I can just save Rebecca, I'd want nothing more than to destroy all my notebooks and try to erase all the information from my mind. I know I'm probably a fool, but I keep thinking that then I might be able to at least try to live some kind of normal life. I'd really like to just fade away one day to nothing and be entirely forgotten."

"I suppose it's not much fun being a witch," he suggested.

"And I really don't like that term," she said stiffly, before looking at the notebooks for a moment longer. "But, no, you're right. It's definitely not much fun being a witch."

CHAPTER FOURTEEN

"THIS PART'S FASCINATING," JIMMY said several hours later, still working by candlelight as he looked through yet another of Lydia's notebooks. "I might be misunderstanding, but it's almost as if Old Mother Marston believed she could gain power over life and death. Can you imagine that? Power like that would be..."

His voice trailed off. After a few seconds, realizing that Lydia hadn't said anything for a few minutes, he turned to see that she was asleep in the nearby armchair.

"Poor thing," he whispered, getting to his feet and fetching a blanket from the corner, then carefully placing it over her. "You must be so terribly exhausted. I can't imagine the toll that all of this has been taking on you."

He took a moment to arrange the blanket neatly. Lydia murmured something in her sleep and shifted slightly, but she didn't wake up; instead, she seemed to be lost in agitated dreams, and after a few more seconds she began to whisper something under her breath.

"Talking in your sleep, huh?" Jimmy said, before leaning a little closer as he tried to make out the words.

"Father, I'm sorry," she was muttering. "Father, please, you have to forgive me."

He waited as she let out a faint whimpering sound.

"Father, I'm begging you," she added, furrowing her brow while keeping her eyes clamped tight shut. "You have to believe me, it was all a mistake, I..."

She groaned briefly, and then she fell silent while still twitching slightly.

"Sweet dreams," Jimmy said softly, before moving a strand of hair from across her face. "Or nightmares, as they seem to be. I just hope -"

"Help me!" a voice called out.

Startled, he turned and looked toward the hallway. His mind was racing, but the voice had sounded like a younger girl, and after a moment he realized that it had come from somewhere upstairs.

"Please help me," the voice continued. "Don't let her wake up. Please, you have to help me before she hurts me again."

Looking back down at Lydia, Jimmy saw that she was still asleep and still seemingly locked into some kind of nightmare. He made his way to the hallway and looked up the stairs, but he already knew that the voice was coming from the spare bedroom, which meant that it could only belong to one person. Feeling a growing sense of dread, he walked to the bottom of the stairs and looked up, but after a moment he realized that he needed help; although he didn't want to disturb Lydia, he turned to go and wake her so that -

"Wait!" the voice upstairs hissed. "Please don't! She doesn't sleep often. This might be my only chance to get away."

Standing in the middle of the hallway, Jimmy looked back at the stairs once more.

"She's torturing me," the voice continued, sounding as if it was about to break into a series of sobs. "I can't bear it, I just want to be free. Everything she told you was a lie! Please, won't you help me?"

***

Reaching the bedroom, Jimmy found that the door was now open. He pushed it a little further, and he immediately saw that Rebecca was staring at him from the bed.

"Thank you," she gasped. "I honestly didn't think that you'd listen. I thought she'd managed to trick you with her cruel falsehoods."

"She's trying to help you," he replied.

"No, she's really not," she said, and now she sounded increasingly desperate. "She wants to use me for her experiments. She reads those books all day and all night, and then she tries things out on me. She takes my hair, or sometimes my skin, even my blood. I'm barely aware of what's going on half the time, it's almost as if she's trying to tear me apart. She's a witch and she uses her powers for terrible things, and I just want the pain to stop."

She hesitated, and now the milky white patches faded from her eyes. At the same time, a little more color returned to her features and she began to look almost healthy.

"If you won't release me," she continued, "then will you at least kill me?"

"I'm sorry," he replied, turning to walk away, "but I think -"

"I'm begging you to put me out of my misery," she added, causing him to stop again. "One way or another. I get it, you're too scared to let me go free. You seem like a decent man, and you're caught up in something that you probably barely understand, but I'm begging you to see through the madness and see that there's only one right thing to do here. Please, you have to make the right choice because otherwise you'll be taking her side. And you wouldn't want to do that, would you?"

"I'm going to fetch Lydia and -"

"And give her another chance to poison your mind?" she sneered. "Then you might as well walk away and pretend that none of this ever happened." Tears were running down her face now as she pulled again on the chains. "I only wanted to learn. Is that a crime? I wanted to learn the things that she knows, and instead she decided to use me to test out all her crazy ideas. I know you think she's a good person, but how well do you really know Lydia Smith?"

"I... know her well enough to be able to say that she's a good woman," he said cautiously.

He waited, but after a moment he heard Rebecca starting to laugh. As he turned to her, he saw a delirious smile spreading across her face, although after a moment she broken into a series of hacking coughs. These coughs continued for a few more seconds, until Jimmy instinctively hurried into the room and grabbed a glass of water from the table, holding it out so that the girl could drink.

Spluttering frantically, Rebecca leaned closer and took some sips.

Watching her, Jimmy sat on the edge of the bed and couldn't help but notice that the girl was in the most awful state. Her hair was matted and dirty, and sores covered her skin; the room was filled with a terrible stench that he could only assume came from the dirt that had been allowed to dry into the bed-sheets, and after a moment he spotted a metal bucket near the bed filled with what appeared to be some very dark urine. In fact, the more he looked around the room, the more Jimmy began to wonder just why the poor imprisoned girl had to be kept in such an awful state. Even if all Lydia's claim held true, could she not at least hold Rebecca in a more dignified condition?

"Thank you," she gasped, finally pulling back from the cup. "I'm sorry about what I said just now. I'm just scared, that's all, but I can tell you're a good man. I know I'm asking you to believe a lot."

"It's not that," he replied, "it's just... I've done some research into these matters in the past, but I'm by no means an expert. At the end of the day, I have to trust Lydia."

"That's exactly what I thought once, too," she told him, and now her bottom lip was trembling slightly. "Now look at me. You know, I think she's damaged from something that happened to her in her childhood. I heard a rumor once that she kept her own mother in much this same condition, trapped in a bed and unable to leave."

"I'm sure that's not true."

"Perhaps you're right," she continued, before leaning closer as the chains rattled gently around her, "or perhaps she's just taking advantage of the fact that you're a good-hearted gentleman. Have you considered that possibility, Mr. Ward? Don't they say that evil forces often seek to manipulate those with righteous souls? Don't they say that evil forces *enjoy* destroying the good?"

"I really wouldn't know about that," he stammered.

"And it happens all the time," she added. "If I die here, chained to this bed after countless experiments, that won't even be remarkable. Evil triumphs so often in this world, Mr. Ward, that the only truly surprising thing is when occasionally the opposite happens. But I suppose I shouldn't have dared hope for that, since it was always going to be so very unlikely. I'm so sorry to have troubled you with my requests for helps. Go downstairs, listen to Lydia's lies and don't strain your mind by trying to think too much about them. It's so much easier, after all, to accept a comforting falsehood than it is to face the truth. I don't blame you for your weakness."

"It's not weakness," he replied, shocked by her claim, "it's merely a case of -"

Stopping suddenly, he thought for a moment about everything she'd just said.

"My name," he added cautiously. "How did you know my full name?"

"I'm sure you must have mentioned it, Mr. Ward," she replied, before reaching over and touching his hand. "Let's not focus on the unimportant details. It's a shame you're going to side with the witch, because I think you and I could have had so much fun together. You're a strong, intelligent and – dare I say it – handsome fellow." She moved her hand toward his wrist. "In another life," she whispered, "I think we could have been very good for one another."

"I should go now," he replied, as he felt himself starting to sweat profusely.

"Just give me one last moment," she said desperately, before starting to lean toward him. "Please, I just -"

Suddenly she let out an anguished scream, more like the sound of a frantic cat, and Jimmy pulled back as something sharp slashed against his face.

CHAPTER FIFTEEN

"WHAT THE -"

Startled awake, Jimmy found himself sitting at the desk in Lydia's front room. Smythe was sitting on the desk and glaring at him, with one paw raised, and after a moment Jimmy reached up and felt a small amount of blood dribbling from a set of slight cuts on his cheek.

"Ah, good," Lydia said, and he turned to see her sitting on a chair in the far corner. "You were asleep. I didn't want to wake you, not after all the work you've done this evening, but... Well, Smythe rather stood guard over you. I hope he didn't hurt you."

"No, it's fine," Jimmy murmured, wiping the blood away before looking at Smythe and once again seeing an intense, almost accusatory expression in the cat's eyes, as if it had been reading his dream. "I was just... dozing, that's all."

Smythe let out a faint hissing sound.

"Leave him alone, Smythe," Lydia called out, and the cat immediately jumped down off the desk. "He's a wonderful cat," she continued, as she looked through another of the notebooks, "but I rather fear that he's slightly possessive. Well, if you'd been through some of the things that he's been through, I'm not sure that you'd be a big fan of other people either."

"He certainly seems protective," Jimmy murmured, wiping a little more blood from his cheek as he stepped around her and looked down at the images in the notebook. "A ducking stool. Even by the standards of today, that seems excessively old-fashioned and brutal."

"Yes, it was," Lydia said softly.

"I beg your pardon?"

"I feel like I'm starting to forget things," Lydia continued, before taking a moment to rub her eyes. "That's new, I always assumed that I'd remember everything from Old Mother Marston's books forever, but now parts of my brain feel rather foggy."

"You're tired."

"I've been tired before."

"How many hours do you sleep each night?"

"I sleep as much as necessary, and no

more."

"That might not be enough," he replied. "Lydia, you're going to be no use to anyone if you keep pushing yourself to the limit. I happen to have some free time, so would you consider letting me stay for a few days, so that I can help you a little more?" She looked up at him. "I can find a room in the village, if you're worried about people gossiping."

"I think I'm way past that point," she admitted with a faint, tired smile. "But I can't drag another innocent person into this situation. This whole problem arose precisely because I let someone in when I shouldn't have. I'm not going to rectify that now by doing the exact same thing again."

"Or you could argue that the problem arose because you never accepted any help," he argued. "I'm not suggesting for one moment that I should take over, but I know a lot about folk legends from this part of the country and I'd genuinely like to see if I can help you out. If you really want me to leave at any point, you can throw me out, but can't you at least try to let me help?" He paused, waiting for an answer. "Who knows?" he added. "I might *actually* be able to offer a fresh pair of eyes. What do you say?"

***

A short while later, having climbed into a single bed in one of the spare rooms upstairs, Jimmy settled back against the pillow and tried to get comfortable. He couldn't help but think about Rebecca Barnett in the next room, and although he tried to put the poor girl out of his mind, part of him worried that she was suffering in true agony.

Sure, his dream had been 'only' a dream, but he still couldn't shake the fear that Rebecca wasn't being treated very well at all.

Staring at the ceiling, he tried to put all such thoughts out of his mind. He'd already blown the candle out, and he felt utterly exhausted, so he supposed that he probably shouldn't have too much trouble getting to sleep. Part of his mind kept drifting to the thought of Rebecca chained to a bed in the next room, but he very quickly forced himself to focus on other matters. The best way to help but Rebecca and Lydia, he knew, was to get on with the task of studying the various notebooks and trying to understand what had caused the situation in the first place.

He had faith in his own ability to get to the bottom of the problem, and in the fundamental power of reason and logic to counter chaos, so he carefully folded his hands across his belly and tried to empty his mind.

And then, a few seconds later, he heard a

very faint creaking sound. He looked down toward the bottom of the bed, just in time to see the door gently inching open. He was sure that the door had been shut properly, but a moment later Smythe jumped up onto the bed and immediately began to make his way across the sheets.

"Come to join me, have you?" Jimmy muttered. "Well, I suppose that's alright, so long as you're not a snorer. I'll have to shut that door, though."

He tried to get up, only to find that his entire body was locked rigidly against the bed. He tried again, confused by what was happening, only to realize that he couldn't move at all; every inch of his body below the neck was held securely in place, as if his bones had been replaced by immovable metal rods. The more he exerted himself, the more he felt his flesh and muscles straining against whatever was holding him in place.

Smythe, meanwhile, stepped onto his chest and then sat down, staring into Jimmy's eyes.

"I don't quite know what's going on," Jimmy murmured, trying to pull first one way and then the other. "It's as if-"

As he continued his efforts, his chest barely moved at all, and Smythe certainly showed no sign that he was in any way uncomfortable. A moment later, however, the cat lifted up a single paw and slowly extended his claws.

"I can't move," Jimmy said, trying not to panic. "Is this some kind of spell?"

Smythe tilted his head slightly, watching Jimmy's eyes at first before looking instead at the man's nose. Clearly untroubled by the struggles beneath him, Smythe blinked impassively and then looked at Jimmy's mouth, and here his gaze lingered as if he was trying to come up with some kind of plan.

"This is the most unusual thing," Jimmy grunted. "I've never been immobilized like this, it simply beggars belief. Is there some kind of sickness that can leave a man in this way?"

Very slowly, Smythe moved his paw toward Jimmy's mouth, making sure that his claws were ready to hook onto the struggling man's lips. Purring slightly, the cat seemed utterly focused and unaware of any -

"Smythe?"

Hearing Lydia's voice calling out on the landing, Smythe turned and looked over at the doorway. A fraction of a second later Jimmy – having suddenly regained the ability to move – rolled over and almost fell off the bed entirely, while sending Smythe leaping down onto the carpet.

"Smythe, are you troubling Mr. Ward in there? You really mustn't do that."

Sitting up, Jimmy tested his arms and legs to make sure that they worked.

"Smythe, I'm being serious," Lydia continued. "You must come out of there immediately. Do you hear me? I simply won't have you bothering our guest."

Smythe looked at Jimmy for a moment, before slinking toward the door. Stopping once he was outside, he turned and let out a faint hissing sound, before the door bumped shut again.

"I'm so terribly sorry, Mr. Ward," Lydia called through to the room. "I shall make sure that Smythe doesn't bother you again. He's not a bad cat, I promise, but I suppose he just doesn't like having someone else staying in the house. I hope you'll be able to sleep well tonight."

"I shall certainly try," he replied, before listening to the sound of her still muttering away to Smythe, following by the tell-tale bump of her bedroom door closing.

Getting to his feet, he took a moment to double-check that all parts of his body were indeed working properly. He had no idea why he'd briefly lost the ability to move, but he told himself that there was really no need to be concerned. Turning to climb back into the bed, he paused after a moment as he looked over at the door; although he supposed that he was probably being a little paranoid, a few seconds later he hurried across the room and began to push the dresser until it was fully blocking the door.

At least that way, he thought as he went back over to the bed, there was no risk that he might be disturbed yet again by that rather unnerving cat.

CHAPTER SIXTEEN

THE FOLLOWING MORNING, STANDING in the kitchen, Jimmy held up a jar of what appeared to be human blood. Turning the jar around in the light, he saw that there seemed to be spices or some other organic material floating around in the mixture.

"That's Rebecca's."

He turned to see that Lydia was watching him from the doorway.

"She drained it from herself one night when I wasn't paying attention," she continued, stepping into the room. "I've managed to make sure she never does it again, and I must admit that I've used the blood once or twice as part of various... rituals that I hoped would make her well again."

"How did that go?" he asked.

"She's still chained to the bed, is she not?"

Jimmy managed a nervous smile, before looking at the jar of blood again.

"I was just wondering," he said after a moment, "whether you might have been using it to..."

His voice trailed off.

"To keep myself looking young?" she suggested.

He glanced at her.

"I don't blame you for thinking that," she continued. "I'd have thought the same. In truth, I tried a spell... not that I like that word, but I suppose it does the job... and it worked. To look at my face, you'd think I haven't aged a day in many decades. Of course, my mind has aged, but that's another matter entirely." She looked at the blood again. "But that has nothing to do with blood, be it my own or that of anyone else. I might be a lot of things, Mr. Ward, but I am most certainly not a vampire."

"I never suggested that you were," he replied. "Others have, though, I assume?"

"I've used a few parlor simple tricks that I remembered from Old Mother Marston's books," she explained as she took the jar from him. "Believe it or not, keeping oneself young isn't really very difficult for a w -"

She stopped herself just in time.

"For one such as myself," she added

carefully. "As far as I can tell, there seems to be no limit to how long the rejuvenation can last. I have to admit, I often wonder why Old Mother Marston didn't use it herself. As the nickname implies, by the time of her death she was regarded as positively ancient."

"If she could live forever," Jimmy replied, "then... why didn't she?"

"Exactly," she agreed. "I'm sure there's some deep philosophical reason for it, one that's likely beyond my simple comprehension."

"Don't sell yourself short."

"What exactly are we going to do today?" she asked, setting the jar down. "I confess that sometimes around this part of the morning, I rather dread going to the desk and picking up those notebooks again."

"Which is exactly why I propose that we head out," he replied.

"Out?" She paused, clearly nervous. "Where to?"

"Where else?" He watched her face, as if he was trying to read her reaction. "I think we need to go back to where it all started. By my reckoning, Almsford is... what, one hour away by train? How would you feel about returning after all these years?"

***

"Absolutely utterly dreadful," Lydia said later, as she stepped down from the train onto the platform at Almsford Station. "There wasn't a train service here back when I was a girl."

"Now it's part of the main line that runs down from London Victoria," he pointed out, "through here and on to Cobblefield and then the coast. Amazing, isn't it? You could take a day trip from here to Crowford or Margate, and be back home in time for supper."

"The world moves rapidly," she said, as they made their way along the platform and emerged at the top of the hill leading down into the village. "So much has changed," she added, taken aback. "I suppose the opening of the railway line brings more people down from the city."

"Are you sure you're alright to be here?"

"As you pointed out," she replied, "many years have passed since I left. I'm quite sure that nobody here will recognize me." She paused for a moment. "On the way here, I noticed that the railway line now passes right through what used to be Bloodacre Farm. I suppose the land was purchased by the company and they knocked down what was left of the old buildings. Not that there *was* much left, but it's still something of a surprise to see how literally the new world has sliced through the old."

"Are you saddened?"

"No," she said, shaking her head gently as she watched two children running past, and then she began to lead him along the street. "The world *must* change, and it's inevitable that we old fogies won't like that very much but we have no right to try to hold things back. We must simply let the next generations move forward, and support them with good grace, and counsel them where we can. But it becomes their world eventually and that is, I believe, as God intended."

"God?"

"Are you surprised that I can even say that name without bursting into flames?"

"No," he replied, but he was evidently flustered and he took a moment to compose his thoughts. "I mean... a little. I mean, no, but..."

"It's quite alright," she continued, "I understand that you're worried about causing offense, but I'm long past such things. The truth is, I haven't quite settled upon my views when it comes to this matter, and I have accepted now that I never shall."

Stopping for a moment, she looked at the front of the public house.

"Now *this* hasn't changed very much," she observed with a wry smile, as two drunks struggled to stay awake on a bench outside the front door. A post in the window advertised something called the

Almsford Historical Reenactment Society, which was apparently due to hold its big launch night soon. After a few seconds she turned and looked across the village green, and she immediately felt a shudder pass through her bones as she spotted the large tree at the far end.

She felt another shudder as she remembered how her body had been strung up there for the entire village to see. Children had pelted her corpse with stones, women had whispered curses as they passed and she'd even overheard people discussing whether to pull her down and rip her to shreds. She'd been conscious the whole time, of course, not breathing but still somehow alive, listening to everything that had happened around her. Part of her had wanted to free herself and leap down and terrify everyone, yet she'd managed to remain still and silent, preferring instead to wait for a chance to escape. That chance had come later, once she'd been on Mr. Potter's table, but she could still feel each and every cut and bruise that had been visited upon her corpse.

Although she was tempted to hate everyone in the village, she forced herself to remember that they'd merely been following orders. Besides, most of them were dead now.

Spotting movement nearby, she saw an elderly man sitting on a bench. Wondering whether she recognized him, she began to suppose that he might have been one of the young boys who'd thrown stones at her corpse. He was so ancient now, and she couldn't help but notice that his hands were shaking. She pushed away any sense of anger, and after a few seconds she managed to find a few scraps of compassion. And then, slowly, she realized that he was looking at the tree, and she wondered how the events of all those decades ago might have damaged such an impressionable young mind. Had the man's life been changed by those days?

"Lydia?"

Turning to Jimmy, she realized that she'd been lost in a world of her own.

"I'm sorry," she said, "I just -"

Before she could finish, she heard a pained cry. She turned to see that the old man had tried to stand, only for his legs to buckle. She instinctively rushed over and helped him up, setting him back onto the bench before handing him his walking stick.

"Thank you," he stammered, a little out of breath. "You're too kind."

"It's nothing," she replied, looking into his bloodshot eyes and realizing that – yes – this *was* one of the young boys from the past.

"My knees aren't what they used to be," he continued, managing a faint smile. "It's alright for you young things, gallivanting about without any aches or pains. Wait until you're my age!" He chuckled. "No, don't think about that now," he added. "Enjoy your youth while you have it."

"I shall endeavor to do so," she said, before removing one of her black lace gloves and reaching down, briefly placing a hand on each of his knees in turn. "Look after yourself."

"I'll do that," he replied. "You're most kind."

"What was that all about?" Jimmy asked as Lydia slipped her hand back into the glove and headed over to join him. "Someone you know?"

"Absolutely not," she replied, walking straight past him, horrified by the fact that she'd touched the old man's knees at all, hating any kind of human contact. "We came here for a reason, and we mustn't dawdle. I need to be home in time to give Smythe his supper."

CHAPTER SEVENTEEN

"NOW HERE'S ONE PLACE that *hasn't* changed," Lydia said as she stepped into the hallway of Old Mother Marston's cottage. "It's as if not a day has passed since the last time I was here."

"Odd that it's still unoccupied," Jimmy replied, as he pulled the knife out from the lock and followed her inside, before carefully shutting the door. "You don't think... I mean, is it possible that people pick up on some kind of... strange atmosphere here?"

"Do *you* notice anything?" she asked as she reached the bottom of the staircase and looked up.

"It's dusty," he observed as he turned and looked all around the hallway. "I truly believe that nobody has set foot in here for many decades. But if you're asking whether I'm noticing a ghostly presence, then I have to admit that there's nothing so far." He ran a fingertip along a table, gathering a thick layer of dust. "Then again," he added, "I don't suppose that I'm the most observant fellow in the world."

"That's a lovely old table," she said. "I'm surprised my father and I missed it on our previous visit. I'm sure it could have been sold."

"You know a thing or two about furniture, don't you?"

"That was a lifetime ago," she replied softly, with a hint of sadness in her voice. "More than a lifetime."

"You moved away," he continued, "but not so far. Why didn't you go further?"

"This part of the world, of the country, is my home," she told him. "I'm allowed some comforts, am I not? Besides, I hoped that I would be left alone. A few people recognized my name, though. Everything after that was something of a struggle."

"If it had been me, I think I'd have moved to the other side of the world," he suggested. "India or -"

"She's here," Lydia said suddenly, looking up at the landing at the top of the stairs.

"Old Mother Marston?"

"I sense her," she continued, with a hint of awe in her voice. "All these years later, her spirit lingers."

"Well, that's..." He paused. "That's good, isn't it?" he suggested finally. "Isn't that what we came here for? To find her ghost, if possible, and try to get some answers?" He waited for her to say something. "I suppose it's a little cold," he added. "That must mean something, mustn't it? I think I've heard that ghosts can make a place somewhat chilly. In fact, I can almost see my own breath in here. Does that mean that perhaps I'm picking up on something after all?"

"You must wait down here," she replied. "On no account are you to follow me up."

"Of course, but -"

"I need to make that very clear," she added through gritted teeth, as she turned to him. "No matter what happens, no matter what you might hear or *think* you hear, if you come up after me you'll only make things ten thousand times worse. I can handle this, at least I believe I can, but not if I'm distracted. I require absolute focus if I'm to make contact. Do you promise me that you'll stay away?"

"Well, I mean..." He thought for a moment, before nodding sagely. "I promise," he added. "I'll just wait down here."

"No, wait outside," she continued. "Go far away from this cottage. I'll meet you on the village green in around one hour from now, and we can make our return journey from there. Trust me, I know what I'm doing. Now leave me so that I can make contact."

***

Standing at the bedroom window, Lydia watched as Jimmy walked away along the street. She'd struggled to make him understand why she had to be alone, but now to her relief she saw him heading around the corner. Although part of her worried that he might double back at some point, she told herself that for now she simply had to trust that he was a man of his word.

And then, behind her, the old bed creaked gently, just as it had creaked many years earlier when she'd first visited the cottage as a young woman.

"You're still here," she said, keeping her back to the bed. "You don't want me to look at you. I understand that."

The bed creaked again.

"I don't know that you'll remember me," she continued, "but -"

"I remember you," an old, weary voice said, breaking the stillness. "I do not receive many visitors. Especially not these days."

"I -"

"You are the one who took my last book."

"I am," Lydia replied, sensing a little bitterness in the woman's voice. "I only did that because I was curious."

"And how has that gone for you?" the voice asked. "Did your... curiosity work out well?"

"I must admit that there have been certain unintended consequences."

"That is because you were wholly ill-equipped to dabble in these things," the voice explained. "You received no training. No education. You took knowledge that had been gathered over many thousands of years, and you played with it as if it was a mere child's toy."

"That was not my intention."

"Your intention is entirely irrelevant."

"I have always tried to do the right thing."

"And?" the voice asked. "Were you doing the right thing when you incinerated your own father and your home?"

"How do you know about that?"

"I know everything," the voice told her. "Were you doing the right thing when you killed the man who orchestrated your public trial?"

"I was defending myself."

"But you could have let yourself die," the voice snarled. "You could have burned all the books and then removed yourself from existence, so that no-one else would ever have to get hurt. But you didn't do that, did you? Tell me, in clinging to life and bringing about everything that has happened since... do you still believe that you were doing the *right* thing?"

"I came here because I need help," Lydia said, carefully trying to sidestep the question.

"The girl chained in your home, yes," the voice replied. "I know of her. She became lost in the darkness of these powers, didn't she? She became everything you were scared of becoming... everything you worried the Walker girl might become."

"How do I help her?"

"A brick to the head would do the job."

"How do I *save* her?" Lydia asked.

"You can't. Her soul is polluted now, like oil gushing into the ocean. She can't be cleansed, and she can't be separated now from the pure evil that courses through her veins. The only thing you can do, while you have her trapped like this, is end her life. At least that way, she won't be able to hurt anyone else."

"She's only young."

"So?"

"So she should have a chance to live."

"She lost that chance the day she first entered your home and opened one of your notebooks," the voice hissed angrily. "Do you know how long it takes for a soul to become truly lost and doomed? Years? Months? Days? No, it can happen in the blink of an eye, and oftentimes there is simply no way back. I understand why you want to save her, but in truth all you're doing is torturing the poor girl when she longs to be freed from this misery. If you want to do the right thing, you'll go back and kill her as quickly as possible, and then you'll burn her body to ash and pray that no part of her spirit remains. Then, and only then, can you claim to be trying to do the right thing."

"There has to be another way," Lydia replied, with tears in her eyes.

She waited, and after a moment she heard the voice starting to laugh.

"I refuse to believe that she has to die," she continued, although she was starting to feel increasingly frustrated. As the laughter became louder and louder, she felt almost as if she was being mocked, but she quickly reminded herself that she still had the chance to find her own path. She'd hoped that Old Mother's Marston's ghost might help, yet she also knew that there had to be other options. "I won't become like that," she added. "If I did, I'd be no better than whatever evil infects her. I'd be just another killer, I'd be..."

She hesitated, and then she turned to look at the bed.

"I refuse to believe," she added, "that a witch can only bring evil and cruelty into this world. I refuse to believe that -"

In that moment she let out a shocked gasp as she saw the hunched figure sitting on the middle of the bed. Wrapped in blankets, the figure began to sit up, finally lifting its head to reveal a grinning, laughing face with bloodied black eyes. Convulsing with laughter now, Old Mother Marston reached her hands out toward Lydia as if she meant to grab her by the shoulders, and after a few seconds she began to clamber off the bed.

"We all become corrupted in the end," the old woman sneered, as Lydia backed away. "We all let the evil flow through us! And we all realize, eventually, that the only way out is death!"

Lydia shook her head.

"Life is a trap," the old woman continued. "It's a room, and the only way out is through a door, but the door is the most terrifying thing in all of existence. And no matter how long you manage to stay in the room, eventually you must pass through that door, and you must meet all the pain and fear that awaits on the other side."

"No," Lydia replied, stepping back across the room, filled with the urge to run. "I don't believe you. You're wrong."

"You'll realize eventually," the ghostly figure continued, lumbering slowly toward her. "All the innocence and naivety will drain from your soul, and you'll realize that the only way to end that girl's suffering is to cut out her cold, dead, poisoned heart! And make her go through the door!"

CHAPTER EIGHTEEN

"I THINK I HEARD about a witch once," the young girl said, furrowing her brow as she thought for a moment. "We're not supposed to talk about such things, but I think I heard someone say that there was a witch in Almsford many years ago."

"Is that so?" Jimmy asked, having stopped the girl to ask a few questions as he was wandering past some shops near the village green. "I don't suppose you remember what people say happened to her, do you?"

"I think they burned her," the girl replied, before thinking again for a few more seconds. "Yes, that's right, there was a witch and she was caught and burned. Right here on the village green, if I remember the tale correctly."

"Do you remember what her name was?"

"Oh, it was something quite ordinary," the girl explained. "Lydia, I think. Lydia something. Yes, that's right. I'm sorry, I really don't remember the details. I think it happened a very long time before I was even born."

"Margaret!" a woman called out from the doorway of the bakery. "Get back in here! This floor won't sweep itself!"

"I'm sorry, Sir," the girl said, turning and hurrying toward the shop. "I wish I could have been more help."

"No, you were *plenty* of help," he replied, watching as she headed inside and then turning to look across the wide open village green. "It's just like I always tell people," he continued under his breath. "History changes so much in the telling. Some of the basic facts are retained, but after a generation or two..."

Before he could finish, he saw Lydia hurrying out from the end of one of the streets. Surprised that she was finished so quickly, he took a step forward to go and meet her. And then, to his shock, he saw her stumble and fall down onto her knees.

"Lydia?" he shouted, before hurrying after her. "Lydia, are you alright?"

***

"And I told you, it was nothing," she said as they sat on a bench at the train station. "I just felt momentarily... a little weak, that's all."

"But there must have been a cause," he replied. "You still haven't quite told me what happened in Old Mother Marston's cottage. Did you even get to speak to her?"

"Yes," she said cautiously, before pausing for a moment. "No. In a manner."

"What kind of manner?"

"I'm so very tired," she said, wiping her brow. "It was an exhausting few minutes, and I'm afraid I can't give you a blow-by-blow account of exactly what happened, so please don't keep on about it."

"Alright," he replied, glancing along the platform but seeing no sign of the train just yet. He thought for a few seconds, struggling to hold back from asking her more questions. "But did you at least get *some* answers?"

"I got enough," she replied darkly.

"And did those answers help in any way?"

"I suppose they did, really," she told him, with a sense of foreboding in her voice. "It's just that I didn't like what I heard, and now I'm having to decide whether to trust Old Mother Marston or -"

Stopping suddenly, she thought back to the moment earlier when she'd rushed from the bedroom. Desperate to get away from the cackling ghostly figure, she'd almost fallen as she'd hurried down the staircase, and then she'd reached the hallway only to freeze as she'd heard the old woman's final words.

"This train seems to be running a few minutes late," Jimmy muttered, checking his pocket watch. "I might have to go and ask the stationmaster about it soon."

He looked toward the office, and then he turned to see fresh tears filling Lydia's eyes.

"I do hate to press the point," he continued, "but I rather feel as if you and I are in this together, and that I can only really help you if I know what's going on. Given that, I have to wonder exactly what happened to you in that cottage." Again he waited for an explanation, and again he received no such thing. Finally, unable to hide his frustration, he got to his feet. "I suppose I'll just have to go there myself and -"

"No!" she blurted out, reaching out and grabbing his hand. As soon as she felt his touch, she pulled her hands back as if she was horrified by what she'd just done. "Promise me you won't do that. Promise me that you'll stay away. That cottage has to be left alone until its wretched ghost is long gone."

"You have to tell me what she said to you," he replied. "How can I help you if you won't share these things with me?"

Although she heard his voice, Lydia was already thinking back to that final moment in the cottage's hallway. She'd been just about to leave when the old woman's voice had given her one last warning.

"You know I'm right," she'd snarled. "How long will your vanity cause you to deny what's obvious? This is the classic conundrum that eventually trips all of us up. To be good, you must be bad, and to be bad you must be good. You can't have it both ways, young lady. What will you decide?"

"I can't do it," she whispered now, as those words went round and round in her thoughts. "I just can't. I don't have it in me... to be so utterly wicked."

"What are you talking about?" Jimmy asked, as the approaching steam train finally whistled in the distance.

"Why would the world ever be organized in such a way," she continued, having not even heard his voice, "that such terrible things must occur? Why would such horror and cruelty be allowed to exist? It just doesn't make sense, and I refuse to believe it."

"Lydia?"

"There must be some other way," she added, "and -"

Suddenly feeling him touch her hand, she

gasped and got to her feet. Stepping back, she stared at him in horror, but she stepped back again until suddenly she began to topple over the edge of the platform. She turned and saw the train pulling into the station, but at the last second Jimmy rushed forward and pulled her back. They landed together on the platform as the train rumbled past, and for a moment Lydia seemed not to even understand where she was or what had just happened.

"You almost fell!" Jimmy gasped, as he got to his feet and reached out to help her up. "Lydia, whatever has put you into such an awful state? You'd have been killed!"

"I'm sorry," she stammered as the train slowed and came to a halt. Ignoring his outstretched hand, she managed to get up without any assistance. Moments later, a few doors opened as passengers disembarked. "I really don't feel very well," she continued, "and I just want to get home. Can you please help me?"

"Of course," he replied, opening the nearest door for her. "I don't mind admitting, you gave me quite a fright just now."

"Yes, I'm sure," she said as she stepped up into the carriage. "I'm sorry. I'm just not quite feeling like myself at the moment. I think it has to do with being here at Almsford again."

"Are you sure the ghost in the cottage didn't say anything to upset you?"

"Quite sure," she said as she sat down, waiting for Jimmy to pull the door shut. "In fact, Old Mother Marston didn't really appear at all."

"She didn't?"

"I heard a few bumps here and there," she explained, as a man called out to warn passengers that the train would soon be leaving. "Some settling floorboards. Creaking doors. That sort of thing. But nothing worth getting worked up about."

***

As the train departed, a woman made her way off the platform and out onto the street, where she immediately spotted a familiar figure hurrying toward her.

"Daddy!" she called out, rushing over and giving him a big hug. "You didn't need to come and meet me! Your poor knees must be giving you the most terrible pain!"

"It's the strangest thing," he replied, pulling back and giving her a twirl, briefly balancing on one leg before hopping around her. "Look! I don't know what happened! A couple of hours ago they were hurting worse than ever, then I sat on a bench before coming here and... I don't know how, but suddenly all the pain is gone! I'm as good as I was when I first started courting your mother at dances!"

As if to prove that point, he took her by the

hand and shocked her by spinning her round.

"See?" he continued with a huge grin on his face. "The rest of me still aches, but my knees have never felt better! It's a miracle!"

CHAPTER NINETEEN

"LEAVE? BUT... WHY?"

"I'm a single woman living on my own," Lydia pointed out firmly, storming across the hallway at Styre House and pulling the door open, then waiting for him to go outside. "I can't have an unmarried gentleman living here with me! It's wrong!"

"Lydia..."

"What will people say?"

"Well, as you pointed out once before, they've got other worries about you," he said cautiously. "Lydia, listen, ever since we got back from Almsford this afternoon you've been acting strangely. You're clearly not quite right, and it's obvious that you're not being entirely honest about what happened with Old Mother Marston."

"Are you accusing me of lying?"

"I'm suggesting that something has terrified you," he replied, stopping next to her in the hallway. He reached out and put a hand on the side of her arm, but she pulled back; he tried again, and the same thing happened. "I can only help you," he continued, "if you're *completely* honest with me. About what happened today, about Rebecca Barnett, about your abilities, about your past... about everything."

"You've been most kind and helpful," she replied through gritted teeth, "but I would rather work alone now. Thank you for encouraging me to retrace my steps and go back to Almsford today, I never would have done that otherwise and... you've helped me to come to some very important conclusions."

"Such as?"

"Such as that I must be alone," she said firmly, as Smythe watched from the staircase and let out a brief meow. "Rather, Smythe and I must be alone together," she continued, "and we must deal with our problems as a team. I hoped that outside assistance might be useful, but it wasn't, and I'm only sorry that I might have wasted some of your time. That was never my intention and I can only encourage you now to return to London and -"

"Lydia -"

"And forget that you were ever here," she

added, interrupting him. "Forget that you ever met me. Forget that any of this happened. Please, Mr. Ward, I'm begging you to walk away right now." She paused, waiting for him to reply, and then she stepped aside and gestured once more for him to leave. "Mr. Ward, you are no longer welcome in my home," she added, "and I am asking you politely to leave. If you do not do so, I shall be forced to consider other options."

He opened his mouth to reply to her, before stepping outside. Taking a deep breath, he turned to see that both Lydia and Smythe were watching him, although only Lydia had tears in her eyes.

"Please," he continued, "don't -"

"Goodbye, Mr. Ward," she said, struggling to get the words out. "I wish you a pleasant journey home."

With that, she swung the door shut in his face, leaving him standing alone. He stared at the door for a few seconds, as if he couldn't quite believe what had just happened, and then he slowly turned and walked away, making his way down the steps and casting one last glance back at the house before disappearing around the corner.

***

"It's alright, Smythe," Lydia said, standing with her back against the door as tears ran down her cheek,

"I had no choice. He's a good man, and that's why he can take no further part in what's about to happen. I had to send him away."

Sitting on the staircase, Smythe let out a brief meow.

"I can't let him see what I'm about to do," she continued, heading through to the kitchen and immediately opening the drawer containing various knives. As she reached into the drawer, her hands were already trembling. "He'd only try to stop me, because he'd cling to all those beliefs about doing the right thing, the same beliefs that I used to follow." She picked up one knife, before setting it aside and taking another, then another. "I wouldn't be able to explain. I don't even know if I understand it myself. It's just best to remove him from the situation so that he doesn't have to even think about it."

She examined another knife, then yet another.

"None of these are quite right," she stammered, moving some more knives aside so that she could see the rest. "Why do I have so many, anyway? It's as if -"

She let out a sudden gasp as she caught her hand on one of the blades. Pulling the hand out, she saw that she'd cut the side of her palm, so she hurried to the sink and began to wash the blood away. Wincing, she dabbed at the wound with a towel, but for a few seconds the blood seemed to just keep coming.

"I have to set aside my own misgivings," she continued, "and remember what Old Mother Marston told me and -"

Behind her, Smythe meowed again.

"I know!" she screamed, grabbing a pot and throwing it across the room.

The pot hit Smythe, sending him screaming and scrambling across the room until he was able to take refuge behind the table.

"I'm so sorry!" Lydia said, hurrying over to him, only for him to dart away. "Don't be scared of me, Smythe. I'm sorry, I should never have taken my anger out on you!"

Spotting him watching her from behind one of the chairs, she stepped around to reach him, but he pulled back yet again. When she tried one last time, he arched his back and let out an angry hiss.

"Do you hate me now?" she asked, as blood dripped from the wound on her hand. "I wouldn't blame you if you did, Smythe. I've tried so hard and for so long to do the right thing, yet look at me now. I'm standing here and I'm plotting a murder. I can't blame anyone else. I'm fully responsible for putting myself in this situation where I..."

She paused, contemplating the horror of what she knew had to happen next.

"Where I can't win," she added, shaking her

head gently. "I can't do the right thing, because there *isn't* a right thing, not at the moment."

Hearing a creaking noise, she looked up at the ceiling.

"I just have to trust that Old Mother Marston was right. I'm sure she was far cleverer than I could ever be, and better educated too. I thought I could read and study, and that I'd become clever, but I was wrong. Despite all the trappings of learning, at the end of the day I'm still just a stupid little farm girl with delusions of grandeur. I should have never looked in those books. If I hadn't, by now I'd probably be dead after a long life working in the mud at Bloodacre Farm. Perhaps I'd have married some local oaf, perhaps not, and I might have had a few children. I'd have endured a short and brutal existence, but at least I would never have become evil and at least it would be over now."

She paused again, with tears in her eyes. For a few seconds she imagined herself as some old farmer's wife, getting on with the drudgery of her daily routine. She knew that in such a life, she'd be bitter about having never escaped from Bloodacre Farm, but in that moment she would have traded all that backbreaking work and anger for the horror of her life at Styre House.

"Would that have been such a bad life?" she added. "I would never have known about these dark arts, and I probably would have been frustrated and horribly poor, but at least..."

Her voice trailed off for a few seconds.

"At least I wouldn't have had to make such awful decisions," she continued, "and by now my life would likely have been over anyway. I'd be rotting in a grave. That seems like such peace."

After a moment's contemplation, she turned and looked down at Smythe, who was still watching her from the safety of his spot behind the chair.

"I'm sorry for throwing that pot at you," she said, pulling the chair out and reaching down to him once more. "I didn't hurt you, did I? If only -"

Before she could touch him, Smythe darted away, hurrying out of the room and disappearing out into the garden. Lydia watched him go, and for a moment she considered running after him, but deep down she knew that she was only delaying the inevitable. Seeing that the wound on her hand had more or less stopped bleeding, she walked back to the drawer and selected one of the larger knives, and then she forced herself to go to the hallway and up the stairs.

Each step felt awfully heavy, and she wanted desperately to turn around, but Old Mother Marston's words were ringing in her ears and she told herself that she couldn't possibly afford to back down now. She marched to the opposite door and pushed it open, and then she stepped into the bedroom and – while keeping the knife hidden behind her back – she looked down at Rebecca's crumpled form.

CHAPTER TWENTY

AS REBECCA TURNED AND began to sit up on the bed, the chains around her body rattled gently.

"You look different," she told Lydia cautiously, immediately noticing that she was holding one hand behind her back. "Something has changed."

"I'm sorry," Lydia replied calmly.

"You were away for a long time today. Where did you go?"

"That's none of your concern."

"I think it *is* my concern," Rebecca said, with a hint of fear in her voice now. "After all, am I not allowed to worry when my jailer suddenly takes on aspects of an executioner?"

"I've kept you up here for more than ten years now," Lydia reminded her.

"I'm well aware of that fact," Rebecca pointed out. "You set these chains on me, and while some of them are to simply keep me bound to the bed, others are arranged in complex patterns. You were scared about any powers I might already have developed, so you tried to counteract them."

"Of course."

"Your little plan worked, too," Rebecca admitted. "In some ways, at least. I've had to be more... careful with what I can and can't do."

"All of that is about to end."

"Do I get a last meal?"

"I don't see the point."

"You've kept me well fed, I'll admit that," Rebecca said, watching Lydia's arm as it kept the knife hidden out of sight. "You've tended to me as best you could, although I understand that you viewed me as something of a dangerous caged animal. There were many things you were too scared to do."

"I know that I've made mistakes," Lydia replied, "and that I've probably been crueler than necessary. I thought I was doing the right thing but -"

"Let me see the blade."

"Rebecca -"

"Just let me see it, please," Rebecca said firmly. "I have the right to inspect the weapon that's going to be used to cut my throat, don't I?"

Lydia hesitated, before moving her hand out to reveal the knife.

Rebecca opened her mouth to speak, but for a few seconds she could only stare at the weapon. Finally she looked down, and then she put her hands over her face while breaking into a series of sobbing gulps.

"Please don't make this any harder than it has to be," Lydia said, struggling to hold back tears of her own. "I won't be fooled by any of your trickery."

"It's not trickery," Rebecca cried, looking up at her with tear-filled eyes. "I'm just mourning the life I could have led, if only I'd never been tempted by those notebooks of yours. I could have been happy, but instead I let the worst of my desires take control. I thought I knew best, I thought I knew better than anyone else in the whole entire world, but I let my hubris dominate everything."

She wiped some of the tears away, but more were already falling.

"Lydia, will you do me one favor?" she continued. "After you've killed me and disposed of my body, do you promise that you'll make sure nobody else ever copies my mistakes? I know that I can't be saved now, I get that, but do you promise me that you'll find a way to keep others safe? And would you..." She paused, before gesturing toward the side of the bed. "Would you do one more thing for me, Lydia? Would you sit with me just for a moment before you kill me? I'd like to try to remember what it was like before I made such an awful mistake."

"I think I'd better just get on with it," Lydia said stiffly.

"Please?" Rebecca whimpered. "Won't you sit with me for just a few minutes? Doesn't a dying woman get a last request? It's not like I could hurt you. Even if I wanted to, which I don't, these chains keep most of my powers subdued. I just feel as if you and I are two sides of the same coin, and I'd like just a little while longer with you, now that I feel like myself again. Please, Lydia?"

Lydia stared at her for a moment, before taking a seat. She set the knife on her lap, but she told herself that she wouldn't allow Rebecca to delay things for too much longer.

"I wish I could go back to that silly little girl I was ten years ago," Rebecca said, sniffing back more tears, "and tell her that all her curiosity was going to get her into so much trouble. But I was so naive back then, and so foolish. Can you even begin to understand that, Lydia?"

"Yes," Lydia replied, taking a deep breath, not noticing the way that Rebecca's hands were both slowly turning. "Yes, I can understand that very well."

***

The ball rolled gently across the grass, before coming to a halt against a large rock. As the river rushed past under the nearby bridge, Verity Cain hurried along the road and then crouched down to pick the ball up.

And then, as she turned to hurry away and go back to the field where she'd been playing, she froze as she realized that somehow the river seemed to be calling her. She stared at the road, and then slowly she turned and looked over her shoulder. After a moment she walked to the middle of the bridge, while still holding the ball, and she stood on tiptoes so that she could see over the low stone wall.

Below, the river was churning harder and faster than Verity had ever seen before. Even as she watched the water, she realized that the river's current seemed to be getting stronger before her very eyes, almost as if some hidden force had begun to push the torrent along at ever-increasing speed.

Trying to see even better, Verity craned her neck. She was on the very tips of her toes now, leaning over the wall so far that she had to reach out and support herself against the stones.

"Don't you get too close to the river," she remembered her mother telling her so many times. "Water's stronger than you might think, and you wouldn't be the first person to get washed away."

In the space of a few seconds, the river – usually fairly sedate and gentle – had become a gushing rage of water crashing under the bridge and smashing against the muddy banks. Verity had never seen anything so astonishing in all her life, and she couldn't help but marvel at the immense fury of the natural world. Lost in astonishment, she leaned further forward, then a little further still, until finally the tips of her toes left the ground altogether and she began to tilt over the top of the wall so that she could witness the spectacle in all its glory.

"That girl's lacking common sense, if you ask me," she remembered her father saying one night, when he hadn't known that Verity was listening. "I don't know what'll become of her, because she gets herself into so many little scrapes. One day she's going to get herself into one that's too big for her to get out of again."

"You worry too much," her mother had replied. "The girl's got her head screwed on right, and she's still young. There's plenty of time for her to become more worldly as she grows up."

Now Verity was almost horizontal as she leaned further and further over the bridge. She could feel light spray against her face, but the sight of the water smashing relentlessly against the riverbank – and ripping away chunks of mud in the process – was too alluring for her to pull back. All she knew was that she desperately wanted to see just how much damage the river could cause, and already she'd noticed that one of the trees overhanging the river's course was wobbling slightly, as if its roots were become disturbed and perhaps even loosened. Verity wanted to see the tree falling down into the river, with its roots upended, and she began to hold her breath in expectation as the ball dropped from her hand and fell back onto the road.

    So much power.

    So much strength.

    So much -

Suddenly she lost her balance. Tipping forward, she tried to grip the bridge but she was too late. She didn't even have time to cry out as she toppled over the edge and fell down, crashing into the raging river and quickly disappearing beneath its surface.

    Over the next few minutes, the river began to calm, until finally it returned to its usual sedate flow. Mud had been torn from the banks on both sides, but gradually any muddiness in the water was washed away. All the trees had survived the brief onslaught, although a few of them appeared to be a little unsteady. Otherwise there was no sign at all that there had ever been any kind of change. The river flowed as it had always flowed, while up on the road a small ball rolled across the dirt before bumping against one of the larger rocks and coming to a stop.

CHAPTER TWENTY-ONE

"I NEVER MEANT FOR any of this to happen," Lydia said, still sitting on the side of the bed with the knife in her right hand. After a moment she turned to Rebecca. "You have to believe me."

She waited, but Rebecca seemed lost in her own thoughts, with a faint smile on her lips. Finally, realizing that she was being watched, Rebecca turned to her and the smile faded, and she gently relaxed her hands.

"Sorry," she said, blinking rapidly for a few seconds, "I was just thinking about the beautiful nature in this area. What were you talking about again?"

"I want you to know that I hold myself wholly responsible for what has happened," Lydia explained. "I should never have let you in."

"You weren't to know that I'd behave so badly."

"I've always known that the dark arts are tempting," Lydia countered.

"Then why weren't *you* tempted?"

"Oh, I have been," Lydia explained. "So many times. I suppose that I simply saw the awful things that happened to my parents, and the ugliness that was unleashed when the people of Almsford turned against me, so I resolved to avoid anything like that ever happening again. I'm certainly not claiming to be a decent person, I'm just saying that my circumstances were very different." She thought for a moment. "And I feel the temptation still. I feel it pulling me, trying to draw me closer. I could so easily..."

Staring into space, she tried to imagine how it would feel if she let herself dive deep into the powers. She'd always fought that temptation, but she'd never managed to entirely push it away. Instead, she'd found herself constantly having to remind herself of the need to do the right thing.

"I really hope you won't blame yourself," Rebecca said softly, watching her with an intense stare. "After you've killed me, I mean. Once you've cut my throat, you must dispose of my body somehow and then just get on with your life. That *is* what you're going to do with me, isn't it? I'd imagine that cutting my throat would be the quickest way to murder me, even though it'd take several minutes for me to bleed out. Anything else would be even more torturous and -"

She sighed.

"I'm sorry, Lydia, I shouldn't have described it as murder. I mean, that's technically what it's going to be, but I don't suppose that it's helpful for you to think that way. Why don't we think of it as more of a... ritual killing?"

Lydia turned to her.

"Like burning a witch," Rebecca continued, "or drowning her in one of those old-fashioned ducking stools. That's really what you're planning to do to me, in a way, isn't it?" She waited for an answer, but she could already see the doubt and fear in Lydia's eyes. "It's alright," she added. "There's no need to rush. Take your time and murder me when you're ready, when it's best for you."

As those words left her lips, she slowly turned her palms until they were facing the ceiling, and then she began to raise her hands.

***

"You're lucky," the landlord said as he set a heavy-looking set of keys on the bar. "We don't always have a room going at such short notice."

"Again, I'm so very grateful," Jimmy replied. "I'm just sorry that I showed up like this with no warning, but I wasn't expecting to need accommodation tonight and..."

He tried for a moment to work out how he could explain his situation. Glancing over his shoulder, he saw a dozen or so men sitting around drinking in the gloom of the pub; a few of the men were talking to one another, but most of them appeared to be happy wallowing in their own misery.

"I just need to think before I leave," he continued finally, turning to the landlord. "Just rushing off back to London would feel... wrong somehow." He picked up the set of keys. "I shan't trouble you, though. I'll just be in my room all evening, and I imagine I shall be leaving early in the morning."

"Fine by me," the landlord muttered darkly. "We don't get many visitors round here, anyway. That's why the guest room's usually full of stuff that needs storing, but this week I happen to have cleared it out. Like I told you, you're lucky it's available. If you want feeding later, you're more than welcome to come down and my wife'll be happy to knock something up for you. For a small price, of course."

"Again, you're too kind," Jimmy said, turning to head to the stairs. "I just -"

Suddenly all the other men in the pub stood up, as if they'd been commanded by some unseen signal. Jimmy froze, wondering whether he might have missed something, but the men stood in silence for a few seconds before one-by-one starting to make their way to the door. A few of them bumped into chairs as they walked, seemingly not particularly aware of their surroundings, and finally they filed out of the pub and into the street.

"What was that all about?" Jimmy asked, before turning to see that the landlord was following the others out of the building. "Is anything wrong?"

"Wrong, Sir?" the landlord replied, stopping and turning to him. For a few seconds he seemed utterly confused. "Why... no, I don't believe so. We're just..."

He hesitated, clearly struggling to quite work out where he was going.

"It's just, we need to..."

Lost for words, he looked around, and then finally he turned to Jimmy again. Reaching up, he adjusted his collar before clearing his throat.

"As a matter of fact," he continued, "there's an item of business that we've all been meaning to take care of. We've tried once or twice before, but we never had too much luck. Tonight, though, the moment has come for us to get on with it. I can't speak for the others, but I feel as if the idea just popped back unbidden into my mind. If you leave something for too long, it festers, doesn't it?"

"I suppose so," Jimmy replied cautiously,

puzzled by the man's countenance, then watching as he headed outside to join the others.

Left all alone in the pub, Jimmy considered going out to see what was happening, but at the last moment he told himself that there was no point getting caught up in some kind of bizarre local ritual. Heading to the stairs, he began instead to make his way up, and already he was contemplating the next day's travel arrangements. In truth, he knew that his best bet was simply to leave the village and never look back, to try not to even think about Lydia Smith again. He knew that she was never fully going to accept help from anyone, and he told himself that he'd done all that he possibly could.

Once he was in his room, he walked to the window and looked out. He saw the men from the pub walking away along the main street, and he couldn't help but wonder where they were going; he knew that local villages often had strange traditions, but this seemed particularly unusual. For a moment he considered the possibility that their strange behavior might have something to do with Lydia, although he quickly told himself that he really needed to stay out of the matter. She'd been very clear that she wanted no more help, so he pulled the curtains shut before going and sitting on the end of the bed.

"You have to forget about all of this," he whispered, trying to drum that thought into his head. "You have to pretend that you never came here, that you never met Lydia Smith and that..."

For a few seconds, that idea felt utterly impossible. Part of him wanted to rush back to Styre House and find some way to save Lydia, although he knew that she was more than capable of saving herself. She was just a loner, he realized now, and he knew that attempting to force his company onto her would only make things worse.

"Forget that you were ever here," he remembered her saying. "Forget that you ever met me. Forget that any of this happened. Please, Mr. Ward, I'm begging you to walk away right now. You are no longer welcome in my home, and I am asking you politely to leave. If you do not do so, I shall be forced to consider other options."

"Please," he'd replied, "don't -"

"Goodbye, Mr. Ward," she'd said firmly. "I wish you a pleasant journey home."

And then she'd shut the door, leaving him with no choice; he'd left and walked to the village, and now he sat on the end of the bed and reminded himself that Lydia had every right to demand privacy in her own home.

"Good luck," he whispered now, hoping against hope that she might eventually find a path to happiness. "I wish I could have found some way to help you."

AMY CROSS

CHAPTER TWENTY-TWO

"YOU'RE DELAYING," REBECCA SAID, after several minutes had passed in silence. A few seconds earlier, she had gently lowered her hands – again, without being noticed. "You've been delaying ever since you came into the room. I could be dead by now, my body getting colder and stiffer and -"

"Don't," Lydia said firmly.

"Don't what?"

"Don't talk about it that way."

"I'm sorry," Rebecca replied, her voice starting to tremble with fear, "it's just that you're dragging this out and it's becoming unbearable." She paused yet again, before finally breaking down into another burst of tears. "I'm trying to be brave and strong, but I just can't, not anymore! I know it's going to hurt when you do this and I'm terrified! I don't want to die! Please, why do you have to kill me?"

"Rebecca..."

"I'm going to feel the blade cutting through my throat, aren't I?" Rebecca sobbed. "I've tried to act like I'm at peace with this, but it's all a lie! Deep down I'm still just a scared girl who doesn't want to die!" She tried to lean forward; when the chains held her back, she reached out and touched Lydia's arm. "Please don't kill me!" she gasped. "I'll do anything you want, absolutely anything, I'll even stay up here happily and never complain again! Just don't kill me! Please, Lydia, anything but that!"

Lydia pulled her arm away, before getting to her feet. She still knew that she had to go through with the awful act, yet she was starting to think that perhaps she needed more time to think; she'd promised herself that she wouldn't allow any delays, but now a delay seemed to be the only humane solution. In that moment, the idea of cutting the throat of this sobbing, terrified girl was just too horrible to contemplate.

"Please!" Rebecca whimpered, with tears and snot running down her face. "I'll literally do anything you want if you'll just spare me!"

"It's for the best," Lydia replied.

"Whose best? Not mine! And not yours, either, because your soul will be destroyed forever if you murder me like this in cold blood!"

Lydia shook her head.

"Fine, then do it!" Rebecca replied, turning as much as she could, then reaching up and pulling the back of her nightshirt down to reveal the bare skin at the top of her back. "Cut my head off if that's what it takes, just get it over with quickly!"

Lydia hesitated, before stepping forward and kneeling on the bed. Reaching around, she placed the knife's blade against Rebecca's throat and began to push, and then she sliced across from one side to the other. Looking down, however, she quickly realized that she hadn't pressed hard enough and that she'd succeeded only in leaving a faint red line.

"Do it properly!" Rebecca cried, as her body began to convulse with a series of sobbing cries. "What's wrong with you? Get it over with!"

"I'm sorry," Lydia whispered. "Truly I am, but this is the only way."

She pressed the blade against the girl's throat again, determined to cut so much deeper this time. She began to slice the knife across the flesh, but after a fraction of a second she felt the metal starting to cut through the skin; she instinctively pulled back and threw the knife across the room, sending it clattering against the wall and falling to the floor as she backed away against the window.

Reaching up with a trembling hand, Rebecca touched her throat for a moment. When she pulled her hand away, she saw only the tiniest bead of blood.

"You coward!" she cried out. "You should have done it by now! I need more pain to make me strong!"

"I'm sorry," Lydia replied, shaking her head, "but -"

Before she could finish, she heard loud voices shouting in the distance. She turned and looked out the window, and to her horror she immediately saw a dozen or so men making their way toward the house. Their faces were filled with anger, and a couple of them briefly stopped to pick up rocks from the garden before approaching the front door.

"No!" Lydia gasped, turning and racing from the room. "Not again!"

"What's happening out there?" Rebecca whimpered, but a smile quickly reached her face just as soon as Lydia was out of sight. "Oh dear," she added, slowly clenching her fists. "Have my reinforcements arrived?"

***

"What are you doing here?" Lydia shouted, sliding the bolt across on the inside of the door just as one of the men grabbed the handle and gave it a turn. "This is private property!"

"You know why we're here, Lydia Smith,"

David Overton sneered, trying the door again. "You're a witch and we're sick of having you in our midst."

"This is private property," she said again, unable to hide the sense of panic in her voice, "and I'm warning you that you must leave immediately!"

"Or what?" David sneered. "Are you going to use your powers on us? That won't work this time, because we've come prepared. We're going to document everything that happens so your evil can be proved to everyone!"

"I don't -"

Before she could finish, a bright light flashed in her eyes. Shocked, she turned and saw that one of the men had set up a camera on a tripod in the garden, and evidently he'd just taken her photograph. Realizing that these men seemed much more organized than the rabble that had attacked the house before, Lydia took a couple of steps back as she began to try to work out how she could ever defend Styre House against so many people.

"Are you going to let us in," Martin Compson called out, "or are you going to make us force our way through this door?"

"If we have to force our way in," another man added, "then we'll be all the angrier when we finally get our hands on you. Does that sound like something you want to happen?"

"What I want is for you all to leave me

alone!" she sobbed. "I've never done anything to any of you!"

"What about Rebecca Barnett?" David asked. "You killed her all those years ago, didn't you? Admit it, you probably used her corpse for one of your sickening rituals."

"No," Lydia cried, shaking her head. "I didn't hurt her."

"Then where did she go?" David shouted. "You were going to do something to poor Verity Cain as well, weren't you? It's a miracle she escaped from your clutches!"

"She didn't escape from anywhere," Lydia replied. "I walked her home!"

"A likely story!" another man snarled. "You need to open this door right now, or you're liable to make us all very angry and then we won't be responsible for our actions!"

Lydia opened her mouth to tell him again that he had to leave, but at that moment she heard the sound of glass breaking. She turned and saw that a man had smashed one of the windows in the front room; rushing through, she grabbed a broom and used it to beat his arms as he tried to reach into the house. The man quickly retreated, but Lydia's heart was racing now as she stepped back and heard the sound of angry men making their way around the property. She knew that she couldn't possibly defend the entire place, and that soon they'd find a way inside, and already she was starting to wonder whether she should simply run away.

"Witch!" another man yelled at the front door, banging hard against the wood. "We don't want you here!"

"You're poisoning our homes!" yet another man called out, and now the voices seemed somehow to be ringing out from all around, merging into one furious cry of rage.

Turning to look toward the hallway, Lydia realized that she could barely separate the voices from one another; instead they were merging into a wall of noise and she began to feel as if the entire house was starting to shake. She fully expected to hear more glass breaking at any moment, followed by the sound of the angry mob clambering into the house. Although she had no idea exactly what they meant to do to her, she knew that this time she'd be unable to fight back, and that for some reason they'd chosen this as the moment when they were going to get rid of her once and for all.

Above, the ceiling creaked slightly, as if Rebecca was shifting her position on the bed. A moment later another noise rang out, and Lydia realized that the girl was starting to laugh. Although she wasn't quite sure how, she was starting to understand that in some way Rebecca had managed to bring the angry crowd to the house and was controlling them almost like puppets.

"It's happening again," Lydia whispered, thinking back to her experience on the ducking stool all those years earlier. "I can't ever escape it. They're never going to stop until I'm dead."

CHAPTER TWENTY-THREE

SITTING IN HIS ROOM upstairs at the local pub, Jimmy tried yet again to focus on his work. He'd set himself up at the desk, where he was writing by candlelight. He'd been hoping that he might be able to distract himself by jotting down some thoughts about another project at the library, but – as the candle continued to flicker – he found himself once again thinking about Lydia.

Finally, letting out a sigh, he leaned back in the chair and tried to think of some other way to refocus his thoughts. He reached up and pinched the bridge of his nose. He knew he was too tired to work, but at the same time he was also too alert and wired to sleep.

"Just focus," he whispered, trying a last-ditch effort to regather his thoughts. "You're normally so good at this. Empty your mind completely and then focus on your work. You've done it before and you can do it again."

He sat completely still, with his eyes closed, and slowly he felt all his concerns starting to fade away. After a few more seconds his mind seemed almost entirely blank, and he felt as if the silence was allowing him to reset his brain. He took some deep breaths, and at last he was starting to bring order and control to his previously addled thoughts.

And then, out of nowhere, he heard the sound of a cat's meow.

Opening his eyes, he looked around the room, but he already knew that the meow had come from somewhere outside. He turned and looked at the door, but a moment later he heard the meow again, and this time he headed to the window and looked down into the street.

"Smythe?" he whispered, as he saw a familiar black cat sitting on the ground and staring up at him. "What are you doing here?"

He fumbled for a moment with the latch before opening the window and leaning out into the cold evening air.

"Smythe?" he said again. "Is that actually you?"

As if to answer his question, the cat meowed again.

"You're wasting your time," Jimmy said

firmly, shaking his head. "I don't know what you think you're going to achieve by coming here, but you should just go home. Or go and find a field so you can catch some mice. Just... leave me alone."

He heard the cat meowing again as he shut the window, and then he closed the curtains and waited. He counted to ten, and then – unable to help himself – he slowly pulled the curtains open again and looked outside; to his immense relief, he saw that Smythe was now gone. In fact, rolling his eyes, he realized that the cat probably hadn't even been Smythe in the first place. After all, one black cat looked more or less exactly the same as any other.

Turning to go back to the desk, he froze as soon as he saw that Smythe was now sitting on his papers, glaring at him with an intense expression. Before he had a chance to say anything, Smythe let out another meow, and this time Jimmy knew that the cat meant business.

"What is it?" he stammered. "Smythe? What do you want?" He paused. "Is something wrong with Lydia?"

***

"This is utterly ridiculous," he said a short while later, as he made his way along the road far beyond the edge of the village, with Smythe walking a little way ahead. "Following a cat of all things, with no need to -"

Stopping suddenly, he realized that he could see Lydia's house ahead, but that something was indeed wrong. He squinted, trying to better make out the movement he could already see at the top of the steps, and finally he realized that a group of men appeared to be banging on the front door. As that realization spread through his bones, he also began to hear the sound of the men shouting and jeering, and he understood finally that an angry mob appeared to have arrived at Styre House.

"The fools," he whispered, hurrying ahead, desperate to make sure that Lydia was alright. "The mindless, fearful fools. They're no better than cavemen!"

As he reached the steps and began to make his way up, he barely even noticed that Smythe was darting off into the undergrowth. Instead, as he got to the front door, he saw a man angrily banging on the wood while two others were shouting at a nearby window.

"What are you doing here?" he asked.

David Overton turned to him.

"We're getting this witch out of here!" he snarled, his bloodshot eyes filled with rage. "It's about time!"

"We've waited for too long for this moment," another man hissed, and Jimmy turned to see that this was the landlord from the pub.

"Rebecca Barnett went missing ten years ago and..."

His voice trailed off for a moment, and he seemed a little puzzled.

"And Verity Cain," he added cautiously, before turning to the others. "Verity Cain is missing!"

"Are you sure?" Martin Compson asked. "How do you know?"

"I just... know," the landlord continued. "Somehow."

"He's right," another man added, stepping around from the other side of the house. "I felt it too. I don't know how, but suddenly I know that..."

"She was out playing this afternoon," one of the others said, followed by a murmur of agreement from the gathered mob. "We've all seen her throwing that ball around so many times in the past. She went out with it, and now she's gone. I don't know where she is, I don't know if they've found her yet, but she's just... gone."

"Are you all losing your minds?" Jimmy asked. "You must be making this up. You're acting as if this information has been somehow... beamed into your heads."

"We know what we know!" David snapped angrily, stepping toward him and clenching a fist. "Why aren't you on our side? Are you a friend of the witch?"

"I'm no friend of an angry mob, that's for

sure," Jimmy told him. "You're acting like primitives, like complete fools. Don't you want to be better than this?"

"We want to keep our homes safe," Martin sneered. "We want to keep our *children* safe!"

"Yes, but this isn't the way to do it," Jimmy replied.

"What would you know?" a man nearby asked, before picking up a metal bucket from the garden and throwing it, smashing one of the windows. "Enough talk! We came here to do a job, so why aren't we doing it? Let's get the witch! For Rebecca, and for Verity!"

Jimmy tried again to reason with them, but already they were shouting and jeering again as they attacked the cottage. Watching the scene with a growing sense of horror, Jimmy felt utterly powerless until slowly he began to realize that one rather strange thing was happening. The men were banging on the door and smashing the windows, yet none of them had actually tried to get into the house. The smashed windows afforded them a perfect opportunity to swarm into Styre House, and he knew that Lydia would be unable to fight off so many attackers, yet for some reason the mob seemed determined to not actually go through with the next stage of their plan. They seemed completely oblivious to the fact that they could actually get into the house.

"Something rather strange is going on here," Jimmy muttered, slipping past some of the men and approaching one of the broken windows.

He took a moment to knock some large shards out of the frame, and then he carefully climbed through into the house. Once he was inside, he turned and saw that the men were still banging on the door, and a moment later one of them broke another window, yet still they seemed unable to get past this first stage of their attack. The more he watched them all, the more Jimmy felt as if they were in some way stuck in an early phase of their anger.

"This isn't normal," he whispered, as a shiver ran through his body. "This isn't right."

"They want my blood," Lydia said, and he turned to see her standing in the corner, almost entirely hidden away from sight as she clutched a broom. "There's no going back, not this time. I just have to set everything right first."

"What are you talking about?" he asked, stepping over to her as the angry mob continued to scream and yell outside. "Lydia, they're attacking the house but they're not coming inside. What's going on here?"

"It's Rebecca," she explained, her voice tense with fear. "She's more powerful than I ever realized, and now... I know what I have to do, but I'm too weak. Jimmy... I have to kill her."

CHAPTER TWENTY-FOUR

"WHEN I RESTRAINED HER with the chains," Lydia said, stopping in the hallway and looking up the stairs, "I used a spell from Old Mother Marston's books to contain her powers."

She paused, still clutching the broom.

"I hate using words like 'spell' and 'witch', but I suppose I have no choice now," she continued. "It worked, but perhaps not as well as I'd hoped. I've been feeding her and keeping her alive, and now I realize that perhaps I've only been making things worse. The chains have slowed her down, of course, but she's still been managing to grow stronger over the years. She's been very patient."

"Are you sure that you have to kill her?" Jimmy asked, as a man banged his fists on the door nearby. "Is there no other way?"

She paused, watching the top of the stairs, before shaking her head.

"This whole situation just seems so... barbaric," he muttered. "But why has she brought the mob here? What's the point of that?"

"I imagine that she's too weak to bring them inside," she explained, "so for now, this is as much as she can manage. She wants them to break in and free her, but I've already countered that by putting a spell on her room so that... even if they broke inside, those men wouldn't be able to find her. They'd continually miss the room, they'd notice it but they'd never quite manage to get into it. Even if they did, they wouldn't be able to see or hear her."

"Can't she counter *that* spell?" he asked.

"Perhaps, given enough time," she admitted. "I've always gone by the books, and by my memories of them, whereas Rebecca... she's very different. Her mind is so chaotic. I think she's trying to invent new spells of her own."

"And what does she want?" he continued.

She turned to him.

"If she gets out of here," he added, "and she's free, then what does she want to do next?"

"I dread to think," she told him, "but I imagine she believes she can use her powers with no restriction. I've been such a fool, Jimmy. All these years, I thought I was containing her while I came up with a plan, but actually I've been helping her grow. Meanwhile, she perhaps worries that I might soon be able to take her powers away. That might be why she's trying to strike back at me now. She's too strong, Jimmy. I've allowed her to become like this, and I don't know that I can overpower her."

"You have to find a way."

"There *is* no way!" she snapped, before starting to sob heavily. "It's impossible!"

"Nothing's impossible," he replied, stepping over and pulling her close. For a moment she tried to turn away, but he put his arms around her and held her tight as she continued to cry. "You told me that once. You told me that nothing's impossible, and that anyone who says otherwise is just making an excuse. I know I've barely seen even a fraction of what you're capable of, Lydia, but I have absolute faith in you, and I know beyond a shadow of a doubt that you're stronger than that girl up there in your spare room. You just need to believe in yourself."

She hesitated, before putting her arms around him for a few seconds.

"I'm not strong enough," she whispered.

"Yes, you are!" Pulling back, he put his hands on the sides of her face, forcing her to look at him. "You can end this, Lydia! Just work out how, and then do it!"

She stared up into his eyes, and then she

slowly turned and looked once more at the staircase.

"You're right," she stammered. "At every step of the way with her, I've made the worst choice. All my instincts have been wrong, I tried to teach her and I tried to contain her, but what if..."

Her voice trailed off, and for a moment she seemed lost in thought.

"What if I've been looking at this the wrong way?" she continued. "I need to weaken her first, and I need to become a little stronger, but I think I know how to end this."

"How can I help?" he asked.

She took a step back.

"You can be here when I'm done," she suggested. "If you want to, I mean. But I wouldn't blame you if you left again."

"I'm not going anywhere," he replied.

"Then I'm going to end it today," she continued, with a renewed sense of confidence. "I think I know what to do. I just -"

Before she could finish, the window behind her shattered and two screaming men leaned through. Grabbing Lydia's shoulders, they pulled her back as if they were trying to drag her out of the house. Jimmy rushed over and took hold of her arm, and after a moment Lydia put her hands on the frame and began to push.

"Kill the witch!" David Overton shouted. "Drag her out and burn her!"

With a pained cry, Lydia twisted and pulled free, stumbling away from the window. Jimmy grabbed the broom she'd dropped and held it up as a weapon, using it to beat the men until they pulled away.

"Leave her alone!" he shouted. "Are you so easily manipulated that a girl in chains can turn you into rabid monsters? Can you not even think for yourselves? Look at what you're doing!"

"Give us the witch!" Martin Compson hissed. "That's all we're asking for! Give us the witch and we'll leave!"

"Hopeless wretches," Jimmy sighed, turning to Lydia. "They're not -"

Seeing that she was gone, he looked around for a moment before spotting a patch of fresh blood on the floor. He saw more spots leading through into the front room, so he followed those and to his horror he quickly found Lydia slumped in one of the chairs. The front of her shirt was covered in blood, and she'd already moved part of the tattered fabric aside to reveal a large shard of glass embedded deep in her abdomen.

"The window," she gasped, taking hold of the edge of the glass as more blood ran from the wound. "I wouldn't be surprised if Rebecca..."

Wincing, she began to slide the glass out, only for yet more blood to gush down her belly and onto her legs.

"Wait!" Jimmy said, hurrying over and dropping to his knees just as Lydia threw the piece of glass aside. "You need a doctor!"

"Too late... for that," she said, already struggling to remain conscious.

"Use your powers," he replied. "Use a spell. Fix this!"

"I can't." she said, shaking her head slowly. "It doesn't work that way."

"Of course it does!" he hissed, watching helplessly as she continued to bleed out. "You made yourself stay young, didn't you? So you can fix an injury!"

"It doesn't work that way," she said again, before reaching out with a bloodied hand and gripping his wrist. "Rebecca knew exactly what she was doing. She's weakened me too much now, I don't have a chance of stopping her. Eventually she'll find a way to get out of those chains, and out of that room. Even if it takes her decades, she's too devious to be contained forever." She let out a pained gasp. "I had a good plan, too," she added. "I've ruined everything, Jimmy. I'm a stupid, arrogant fool and I've ruined it all. This is my fault."

"Don't talk like that," he replied, as he saw blood starting to drip onto the carpet. "Tell me what to do, Lydia. Tell me how I can help you."

"There's nothing either of us can do now," she murmured, before pausing for a moment.

"Eventually she'll find a way to manipulate that mob, to get them to break in, and my spell on the room won't last forever in those circumstances. The only thing that would stop them would be..."

Her voice trailed off, and after a moment she sat up slightly.

"The only thing that would stop them," she continued, "would be if they got exactly what they want. Their hatred is their fuel, but what do angry mobs do after they've got what they want?" She turned to him. "They forget. They do everything in their power to forget the awful things that they did. And if they thought they'd got what they wanted here, Rebecca wouldn't be able to lure them back. Her little army would be completely neutralized. That would buy us some time, hopefully enough time to weaken her and time for me to..."

Again her voice trailed off, and after a few seconds she turned and looked through toward the hallway. She and Jimmy could still hear the men shouting outside, and slowly Lydia furrowed her brow.

"But I'm going to need your help," she said firmly, "and I'm going to need Smythe's help too. This plan's a long shot, but it's the only one that might possibly work and I think I remember just enough of Old Mother Marston's magic for us to have a chance. But Jimmy..." She paused, and then she turned to him. "You're not going to like what I need you to do."

CHAPTER TWENTY-FIVE

THE CROWD ROARED AS Martin Compson grabbed Lydia, hauling her out of the house just as soon as she'd opened the door. She stumbled slightly, wincing as more blood ran from the wound on her belly, and then she recoiled as the nearby camera flashed on its tripod.

"We have the witch!" Martin shouted, causing more cheers and cries to erupt. "Now let us end her reign of terror!"

"What are you going to do with her?" Jimmy asked, stepping out of the house with all the color having drained from his face. Already he could see that some of the men had begun to dig an impromptu grave in the garden. "Please, she's already dying."

"You don't need to worry now," David Overton said, placing an arm around him and hugging him tight. "You're a hero to all of us for dragging the witch out of that place. There are no more in the house, are there?"

Jimmy turned and looked back into Styre House. He thought of Rebecca Barnett up in the spare room, and then he turned to David. Every fiber in his body told him that he was doing the wrong thing, but he knew he had to obey Lydia's instructions to the letter.

"No," he lied, horrified by the jeers he was hearing all around. "No, there's nobody else left in there."

"Put her in this!" another man yelled, as he and two others finished banging nails into a makeshift coffin that they'd made from some loose timber found at the end of the garden. "We should contain her evil and make her suffer down there! But be warned, she might try to confuse us with her words. Silence her!"

"What are you going to do to her?" Jimmy asked again.

Two of the men placed a gag over Lydia's mouth, while another bound her wrists.

Her terrified eyes darted from side to side as she watched the mob.

"We'll leave her fate to God," Martin sneered, as some of the others manhandled Lydia across the garden and then forced her down into the coffin. "And the worms. She'll be judged accordingly, but first she'll have ample time to think about all the misery she's brought to the world."

Lydia tried to climb out of the coffin, but one of the men kicked her hard in the face before shoving her back down. More and more blood was soaking her dress, and a moment later the coffin was picked up and tilted so that it could be lowered into the grave.

"No!" Jimmy shouted, rushing forward, only for two of the men to hold him back. "You can't bury her alive! That's monstrous!"

Lydia merely stared back at him, watching his face with a fearful expression as the camera flashed again.

"No, this wasn't part of the plan!" he yelled, but he was powerless to help as the coffin was dropped down hard into the grave.

"What plan?" Martin asked.

"I -"

Realizing that he should say no more, Jimmy fell silent for a moment.

"We thought... I mean, *I* thought that you were going to just... kill her first."

"And burn her, as they did to witches back in the day?" Martin replied. "Or drown her? I think we're past that sort of thing now." He and the others began to assemble around the grave as Lydia wriggled furiously in the coffin as if – even now – she was trying to get free. "We're not savages. As I already said, we'll let the Lord deliver judgment."

"Look what I found," one of the other men said, dragging a stone across the lawn and throwing it onto the grass, then kneeling and taking out a chisel. "It was round the back of the garage. I think it's an old mile marker, but give me a few minutes and I can turn it into a gravestone." He started chipping away at the surface. "Even a witch should have some kind of stone to mark the spot where she was buried. If nothing else, it can serve to keep other people away."

"This is wrong," Jimmy whispered, horrified as he watched some of the men starting to shovel dirt into the grave. "I don't think I can watch this, it's all so..."

Stepping forward, he looked down into the grave. He saw Lydia's terrified eyes, but he realized that she'd stopped struggling now. He had no idea whether her earlier attempts to escape had been genuine, perhaps the result of last-minute panic, or whether they'd merely been part of her effort to convince the men that she wasn't willingly submitting to their punishment. Either way, as he saw her body gradually disappearing from view beneath rocks and dirt, he felt a shiver pass through his soul.

"There's one spell I might be able to use," he remembered her having told him earlier. "This body of mine is dying, but I can preserve it for a while and perhaps later steal... or borrow... another."

"What other?" he'd asked. "What are you talking about?"

"I'll wait down there until the time is right," she'd explained. "I'll know when the moment has come. Smythe can be my guide, he can tell me. Meanwhile Rebecca will get weaker and weaker, hidden away in that room. She'll starve, but she'll manage to keep herself alive. And when the time comes, when I'm able to take the right new body and go back to face her, I know exactly what I must do."

Another shovelful of dirt fell into the grave, and now Lydia was completely covered.

"How long will it take?" he remembered asking her just before they'd stepped out to face the mob. "How long will I have to wait to see you again?"

"You'll be long gone by the time that day

comes," she'd told him, with fresh tears in her eyes. "I'm so sorry. I wish things could be different. Please, just remember what I've asked you to do next, and try to find Smythe too. And Jimmy..."

He remembered that brief pause, and how they'd looked into each other's eyes, and how they'd then leaned closer to each other's faces and briefly shared -

"Done!" David Overton shouted, slapping Jimmy hard on the back, forcing him back to the present. "The witch is buried!"

"How long do you think it'll take her to die down there?" a man asked.

"A few minutes," David sneered. "Then she'll be food for worms."

"I rather think it'll take her a while longer," Jimmy whispered, imagining Lydia trapped down there now in the darkness, dead but aware, condemned to spend decades waiting for her chance to return.

"It's ready!" a man called out, as he and two others hauled the stone across and set it into place. Lydia's name, and some guesses at her dates of birth and death, had been crudely carved into the surface, and a moment later the camera flashed again to record the moment. "It probably won't last forever, but it'll last longer than she does."

"Curse that witch," David said, stepping forward and spitting on the stone. "Curse all the unholy forces in this world."

"Curse her," Martin added, and he too spat on the stone, as did the others one by one. "At least she's gone now. And we've avenged the deaths of Rebecca and Verity."

"You've avenged nothing," Jimmy whispered. "All you've done is make yourselves look like a bunch of murderous barbarians."

"Let's head back to the pub," the landlord said with a grin. "Our work here is done."

"Are you sure we shouldn't burn the house down?" David asked, turning to look at Styre House. "There might be some traces of her evil still here."

"No, there's no need to do that now," Martin told him. "Let's leave it to rot for a while. Eventually someone'll find a use for it, but if you ask me, we should make sure that it's left empty as a reminder of what we did here today. After all, if we forget that we banished a witch, we might let another one slip into our midst."

As the mob began to head away from the house, Jimmy was left lingering in the garden. He desperately wanted to dig Lydia back up and try to find some way to save her, but he knew deep down that he had to let her stick to her plan. He looked down at the grave and imagined her bleeding and sobbing down there, and then he looked up at the house's higher windows and thought of Rebecca Barnett still chained to the bed. Part of him wanted to go up there and finish her off, but Lydia had already warned him that he might succumb to mind tricks. He'd promised to trust Lydia's plan, and he knew now that he had to stay strong.

Turning to walk away, he stopped as he saw Smythe slinking out from the undergrowth.

"Did you see what happened?" he asked, crouching down and stroking the cat. "You might know this already. I don't know how these things work, but just in case you don't... I'm afraid your mistress has a very important job that she needs you to do. You're going to have to watch over the house until she's ready to come back."

CHAPTER TWENTY-SIX

ONE MONTH LATER, SIR Maximilian Withers made his way along an aisle at the library before stopping as he spotted a familiar sight. Jimmy Ward was sitting at one of the desks, furiously scribbling some notes down. Withers watched him for a moment before wandering over.

"Still at it, eh?" he said with a grin. "You're a hard worker, aren't you?"

"I'm just... setting down some local history from a village I visited recently," Jimmy explained. "I think it's important that we remember the stories from these places."

"I suppose you have a point," Withers said, before leaning down to get a closer look. "Where's Styre House?"

"It's in a little village," Jimmy replied, "far

from here."

"And what's this about a witch? I see you've written something about a witch who lived there, but that can't be true, can it?"

"Her name was Lydia Smith," Jimmy explained. "I'm sure the whole story's a lot of fuss about nothing, but according to the locals, she was a witch who..." He took a deep breath, hating the lies he was going to have to tell. "She preyed upon children in the area. There are at least two deaths attributed to her."

"Sounds like a rather dangerous witch," Withers observed.

"Oh, she was, by all accounts," Jimmy said, although he didn't sound terribly sure about that suggestion. "Eventually the villagers rose up and decided they'd had enough. It was all quite brutal in the end. There are various conflicting versions of what happened next."

"I bet there are!" Withers said excitedly. "It's always hard to pin down the truth in situations like that, isn't it? Every man and his dog wants to get his version out, and they rarely match up. So what exactly did they do to this witch, anyway? How did they dispatch her?"

"According to one version of the story, she was burned alive on the village green."

"How terribly gruesome," Withers said, his eyes filling with anticipation as a drop of saliva glistened in one corner of his mouth. "Go on. Are there any more suggestions?"

"Um..."

Jimmy hesitated, before removing his spectacles and trying to ignore a sense of nausea that had begun to churn in the pit of his belly.

"I heard," Withers continued, "that in some parts of the country, they used to flay witches. They'd lightly boil them, just to loosen the skin a little. Then, while they were still alive, they'd whip the witch with a special instrument that would quite literally peel the skin away."

"Indeed," Jimmy replied uncomfortably. "Two young girls went missing near Lydia Smith's home, too. One of them, Rebecca Barnett, was never seen again. The body of the other girl was found washed up several miles away, at least according to one version of the story. Another version claims that she was simply never seen again. Either way, it's hard not to think that Lydia was in some way involved."

"I'm sure she was," Withers said firmly.

"So, in the eyes of many," Jimmy said, "the locals' anger and hatred for Lydia Smith was... justified."

"And in other places," Withers added, "across Europe, they'd put the witch into a big brass kettle kind of contraption and slowly heat her to death over a fire. They say the cries would be heard for miles around. Obviously I'm no expert, but I bet that must have been one of the most agonizing ways to die." He paused. "You don't think... I mean, I don't suppose... do you think they might have done something like that to this Laura Smith woman?"

"One never knows," Jimmy said, as the nausea grew and grew.

"Well, I must be on my way," Withers said, turning and heading along another aisle. "I don't have time to waste, you know."

"Lydia," Jimmy called after him.

"I'm sorry?"

"Her name wasn't Laura Smith," he continued. "It was Lydia."

"Of course!" Withers chuckled with a sly grin. "Always important to get the historical facts right, eh?"

As the older man walked away, Jimmy sat at his desk and tried to pull himself together. After a few seconds, however, the nausea became too much and he rushed over to the bin in the corner; kneeling down, he couldn't help but throw up. A series of painful retches jerked at his stomach; meanwhile his notes remained on the desk, waiting for him to get back to work on a series of fanciful – and very much conflicting – tales about the life and death of Lydia Smith.

***

A little over a decade later, Jimmy Ward – although he went by the name James now, never Jimmy – stopped at the end of the barren country road and looked over at Styre House. Two men were outside the front of the place, working on a motor car.

Spotting movement nearby, Jimmy turned just in time to see that Smythe was making his way over.

"There you are," he said, crouching down and stroking the cat as it came closer and began to brush against his leg. "I had a feeling I'd bump into you here."

Smythe let out a welcoming meow.

"So the place is a boarding house at the moment, is it?" he continued. "That won't last. Do you think..."

He thought for a moment.

"Do you think that's Rebecca's way of trying to be found?" he asked. "Lydia's spell is still keeping her hidden away in that room, but she's trying to draw a succession of people to the house in the hope that one of them might break through and discover her, and then set her free. Is that her plan?"

Smythe meowed again.

"I don't see it working," he added. "I'm sure the house'll fall into ruin long before that. Mind you, I bet Rebecca's rather frustrated trapped in that room, isn't she? I bet she's furious."

Again Smythe meowed, and Jimmy couldn't help but feel that there was a hint of satisfaction in his tone.

"I've done my part," he explained. "I've spread versions of the Lydia Smith story, each completely wrapped up in a load of hogwash. There are so many different versions of the story, even *I'm* struggling to remember which parts are real. I also went to the trouble of getting hold of some of the photographs from ten years ago, and adding those into the mix. I'm confident that any fools who ever bothered to look into the whole thing would get lost in a web of fact and counter-fact until their heads would be positively spinning. That's what Lydia wanted. What she still wants, I suppose."

He paused again, watching as another man emerged from the house to work on the car.

"She's still down there, isn't she?" he continued. "In the dirt. In the darkness. Waiting for her chance to come up and... I must admit, I don't understand every aspect of her plan. I suppose she needs to be strong, and she needs a suitable body she can take over. And she needs Rebecca to get weaker, which might take some time." He patted Smythe's side. "And here you are, playing your role in the whole mess. You don't look a day older than the last time I saw you, Smythe. You're very loyal to your mistress, aren't you?"

With another meow, Smythe brushed against

him once more before starting to walk back toward the house.

"Can't be away too long, can you?" Jimmy said with a faint smile. "Look after her, Smythe. I won't be able to, at least not for a while. I have to go to..."

Stopping, Smythe looked back at him.

"Well, there's a war on now," Jimmy continued, "and I have to go and fight. It's my duty, and I've never shied away from duty." He got to his feet. "So I won't be able to come and check on her for a while. Perhaps I'll make it back in a few years once this ruddy war's over. I might, or I might not. One never knows with wars, does one?" He watched the house for a moment longer, still unable to stop thinking about Lydia buried in that makeshift grave. "Smythe, if I *don't* make it back, then... when Lydia finally emerges, I want you to tell her that I..."

His voice trailed off.

Smythe watched him with a cautious stare.

"Well," Jimmy muttered, almost blushing slightly, "I don't mean to get all sentimental, or anything like that. And to be honest, I don't even know whether I'd live long enough to see her again *without* the war, but I suppose what I'm trying to get at is... I'd like it, if it's not too much trouble, if you could just find a way to let her know that I thought a great deal of her. More than I ever let her know, really."

Reaching into his pocket, he pulled out a small locket. When he opened the locket, he saw a photograph of Lydia's face; the picture had been taken on the day she was buried by the mob, but he supposed that some kind of likeness was better than nothing at all. This was the one image in which she didn't look scared at all; instead, he felt sure that he could see a kind of brave determination as she glared back at the camera.

"The funny thing is," he continued wistfully, "I know that, given the chance, I would have grown to like her more and more. Probably more with each and every passing day for the rest of my life. Not that she'd have wanted me around, I'm quite sure she found me far too irritating, but I would have liked – if she'd given me the chance – to have tried to make her..."

He paused, trying to think of the right word.

"Happy," he added finally, before closing the locket and slipping it away again. "In fact, I would have dedicated my whole life to that aim, given even half the chance. She was quite wonderful, and I think we might have made a good..."

He paused, before taking a deep breath.

"Well, I mustn't stand around all day like this, must I? I've got a train to catch, and then I need to report to the barracks. Hopefully they're going to polish me up a little before they pack me off to fight the Germans." He turned and started walking away. "Keep up the good work, Smythe. And look after her. She might hate to admit it, but she needs looking after now and again. And she deserves it. She deserves it more than anyone I've ever met in my life."

Smythe watched him walk away. After letting out one more meow, he turned and hurried back to Styre House.

***

One year later, a pile of dead bodies lay on a muddy battlefield hundreds of miles away. As shells exploded all around and the ground shuddered, some of the bodies fell from the pile. One body in particular fell in such a way that its left arm dropped down.

The dead fingers opened slightly, revealing a muddy and scratched locket containing the photograph of Lydia Smith. A few spots of blood had fallen on the locket's side. A moment later another shell landed nearby and exploded, showering the pile of bodies with a heavy coating of mud.

CHAPTER TWENTY-SEVEN

Today...

WALKING OVER TO THE window, Colin looked out just in time to see that the bird was still just about alive. Twitching on the grass, the poor thing seemed to be trying to fly again, but Smythe had already made his way over. Colin winced as he saw the cat extend a single claw, which sliced into the bird's chest and lifted its quivering body up from the ground. Smythe stared at the bird as it struggled, before leaning closer and biting its head off, letting blood gush out from the stump.

"Parker," Colin said nervously, unable to tear his gaze away as Smythe chewed on the bird's corpse, "how..."

His voice trailed off for a few seconds.

"He's back," he stammered. "I thought you said he was dragged into the flames. How is he back? When you described it, you made it sound like he'd been dragged down to the depths of Hell."

"Yes," Parker replied airily, "but I wouldn't worry your pretty little head about that too much." She paused for a moment. "He's always had excellent recall."

Colin turned to find her standing right behind him, staring into his eyes with a determined glare that suggested she found something amusing. As he heard the sound of Smythe crunching through the bird's bones outside, Colin stared back at Parker and realized for the first time that he was seeing something different in her eyes. Something colder. Something harder. Something new, or...

Or *someone* new.

"It's so good to be here," she said softly. "You have no idea how long I waited. And now..."

Reaching out, she touched the side of his face, caressing his skin as if she'd been starved of human contact. For the first time in as long as she could remember, she didn't mind the touch of someone else's skin at all; indeed, she actually found the sensation strangely comforting, perhaps because she was using someone else's body. Then again, she remembered being close to Jimmy a few times.

Poor dear Jimmy...

"I won't let them do it to me again," she purred. "This time, if anyone comes to try to take me down, I won't be so patient and I certainly won't show them any mercy." She leaned even closer, as if she was about to kiss him on the lips. "This time," she added, "I'm going to take what's rightfully mine."

She hesitated for a moment, before pulling back slightly.

"I'm sorry," she added, furrowing her brow, "but for a moment there you... I mean, you reminded me of somebody."

"I... did?"

"That doesn't matter now," Parker continued, taking a full step back. "I waited so long, but now I'm finally strong enough, and I suppose she must have weakened terribly over the years." She looked up at the ceiling. "I must admit, I knew it would take a while to reach this point, but I never thought that it would be an entire century. I didn't much enjoy my time down there in that grave. I had far too much time to think, and to go over and over things. I showed so much restraint all those years ago, and I'm not sure – in the same circumstances – that I'd be quite so kind to any mob that came after me."

"Parker?"

Colin waited for her to reply, but a moment later he heard a creaking sound coming from somewhere upstairs.

"There's no-one else here, is there?" he asked, before shaking his head. "Of course not. Why would I even ask such a question?"

"I've been putting this off," Parker whispered, still watching the ceiling. "I suppose a day or two extra didn't hurt, but I really need to get down to business."

"Business?"

"I need you to go outside," she continued, turning to him. "Play with Smythe. Something like that."

"Play with Smythe?"

"Do you have that device you were showing me the other day? The one that seems to somehow... store all the knowledge in the world?"

"You mean my phone?" He pulled his phone out and held it up. "Of course, but -"

"I want you to go outside," she continued, cutting him off, "and look something up for me. That machine seems to know everything, so I want you to look up any record of a man named James Ward. He would have been born, I suppose, around the year 1870 or 1880, something like that. He was a librarian and a history researcher in London. He'll have been dead for a long time now, I'm sure, but he might have descendants or... I'm sure he did something wonderful with his life. Would you mind trying to find out?"

"James Ward?" Colin paused. "It's not the most unusual name, but I can have a go. In fact, it sounds vaguely familiar for some reason but... Parker, why are you suddenly so interested in some guy who was born a century and a half ago?"

"Ask Smythe," she replied with a faint, sad smile. "Now... go outside, Colin. And please, don't come back in until I let you know that it's safe."

***

"Ask Smythe," Colin muttered a few minutes later, as he sat on a low brick wall in the garden and tapped at his phone. "Ask Smythe?"

He turned and looked over at the cat.

"Parker's been acting stranger and stranger since all that... stuff happened. I was thinking that it might actually be over, but now I can't help worrying whether she's still... troubled in some way. I mean, I know she's been through a lot and she must still be traumatized by what happened to her mother, but it's almost as if..."

He thought for a moment longer.

"You're going to think that I'm really crazy now, Smythe," he added, "but when I talk to her, it's almost as if I'm not even talking to the real Parker anymore. It's like there's someone else behind her eyes. I guess this isn't the right moment to talk to her about the book deal."

He looked at the phone and continued to scroll through the list of results on the website. As he'd suspected, there were quite a few James Wards, although so far he wasn't having any luck finding one who'd been a librarian.

"And she says strange things, too," he continued, before sighing and looking at Smythe again. "Am I imagining that, or does she sometimes talk as if she's... going on about things that don't really make sense? She references things that I don't quite get, and also the *way* she talks is quite different. The old Parker could swear like a soldier, but now she seems strangely prim and proper."

He glanced at the house, and after a moment he began to stare at one particular upstairs window.

"Then again," he mused, "I really think that I might be losing my mind." He squinted slightly. "I swear, I don't even get the layout of this house. The window over there is Parker's mum's old bedroom, right? And then there's that window right there, but I've been inside loads of times and I know there isn't a room on that side. There's just... nothing. And then there's Parker's bedroom around the side, and another bedroom or storage room or whatever, and then..."

His voice trailed off again as he tried to make sense of the puzzle.

"So what's *that* room?" he asked. "Like, literally, is there a room there or not? Because on the landing, there doesn't seem to be. And do you know what else is weird? I think I've wondered this exact same thing before, and then I've gone inside to check and sort of... I suppose I always got distracted, and then I forgot, and now I'm sitting here again wondering the same thing and I'm no closer to working it out."

He turned and saw that Smythe had almost finished chewing through the dead bird.

"And now I'm talking to you," he sighed. "Like, I'm literally talking to a cat. How absurd is that?"

He focused on the phone again, not noticing Smythe's disdainful glare, and then he stopped as he came to one particular entry.

"Bingo," he whispered. "Hey, Smythe, listen to this. I've found a record for a James Algernon Ward who was born around the right time, and who worked at a library in London, not too far from Charing Cross." He scrolled down a little further. "There's a photo of him here, and... Well, what do you know? Apparently he wrote a book about local legends from the area. I wouldn't be surprised if he covered the Lydia Smith story. In fact, I think he wrote one that I read quite recently and posted through Henry's letterbox." He scrolled down a little further. "Oh, that's sad," he added. "It says here that he died at the Battle of Mons in the First World War. I wonder why Parker was so interested in him, though, and..."

He thought for a moment longer, before scrolling down to another section and trying to find some more information about the man.

Meanwhile, Smythe sat for a few seconds, watching as Colin continued to work. With a hint of sadness in his eyes, the cat seemed as if he too was lost in thought, as if he was thinking back to that day more than a century earlier when Jimmy had paid his last visit to the house. And then, as if shrugging the whole thing off, Smythe turned and resumed his work on the dead bird, chewing through the corpse and savoring the last of the creature's cooling blood.

CHAPTER TWENTY-EIGHT

AS SOON AS SHE pushed the door open, Parker saw that everything had changed. The spare room's door had stuck slightly, and the hinges had creaked, both of which she took as signs that it hadn't been opened for a very long time. And when she looked into the room, she saw that the previously white walls were now mottled and shaded with patches of what appeared to be some kind of black mold.

On the bed, still wrapped in chains, the horribly emaciated figure of Rebecca Barnett stirred slightly and looked up at her with pure white eyes.

"There you are," Parker said. "Now... where were we, before we were so rudely interrupted?"

"Who's there?" Rebecca gasped, her voice sounding dry and almost crispy. "Wait, your tone is different but I recognize..."

She paused for a moment, before a smile spread across her lips, breaking the dried skin around her mouth and letting blood trickle from the cracks.

"I'd recognize that inflection anywhere," she continued, sitting up a little more as her old bones clicked and groaned while the chains rattled. "Have you finally come back for me, Lydia Smith?" She tilted her head slightly; her pupils could just about be made out beneath the whiteness of her eyes. "You look *very* different. That's not your old body, is it? I'm impressed that you've been able to pull off such a wonderful trick. I wasn't sure that you had that kind of power in you."

"You've been in here for a very long time," Parker replied. "More than a hundred years, in fact."

"I suspected it had been that long," Rebecca admitted. "I certainly tried to attract attention, I cried out so many times, but nobody ever seemed to hear me."

"That was by design."

"I heard that infernal cat on the landing sometimes," Rebecca continued, her face contorting to become a kind of raging sneer. "You left him here as a kind of guard, didn't you? Sometimes late at night, I'd hear him padding about out there on the other side of the door. I called out to him, and he'd stop. He was the only one who ever remembered that I was here, wasn't he? And the only one that ever heard me. When I get out of these chains, and after I'm done with you, he's going to be my next priority. I want to... thank him... for his efforts."

"I didn't come here to catch up with you," Parker replied. "I came to -"

"Oh, to murder me," Rebecca snarled, tilting her head again, causing the bones in her neck to crack. "I almost forgot. Do you have a knife with you? This time are you actually going to go through with it, or are you going to chicken out like last time?"

"I'm not here to murder you."

"Then what are you plotting?" Rebecca asked. "Are you just going to leave me here to rot forever? I kept myself alive, I managed to persist despite the scratching pain of hunger in my belly, but I really don't think that I can keep that up indefinitely. Have you chosen indecision, Lydia? Are you going to leave me here and hope that I just waste away to nothing?"

"No," Parker replied, shaking her head, before making her way around the bed. "I'm not going to do that."

"Sorry about the smell," Rebecca sneered, glancing briefly at the open door before turning to Parker again, looking up into her eyes. "All this mystery and vagueness doesn't suit you," she continued. "Why don't we cut to the chase?"

"I was a bad teacher," Parker admitted. "I let you down, and for that I'm so terribly sorry. I've had plenty of time to think, however, and I've finally realized that it's not too late." Reaching down, she began to gently remove the chains. "What you need, Rebecca," she continued, "is a proper teacher. And with your cooperation, I think I can help you. In fact, I think you have great potential. You might even become more powerful than I ever was."

"You're... releasing me?" Rebecca asked, clearly shocked.

"I am."

Lifting up another part of the chains, Parker found that the metal had begun to fuse to Rebecca's skin.

"I'm sorry," she said cautiously, "this might hurt a little."

She turned one section of the chains around, tearing the metal from the girl's flesh and then lifting it to reveal a bloodied wound with patches of bone showing through. Fresh blood began to bleed out over the blackened crusty areas, and the chains creaked and groaned as Parker carefully lifted some of them over Rebecca's head.

"It feels so strange," Rebecca gasped. "I've been in here for so long, I'd forgotten how it felt to *not* have this burden weighing me down." She sat up a little more, stretching her bones as Parker removed more of the chains. "I truly didn't believe that this day would come, Lydia. I'd almost resigned myself to being beaten by you. I thought I'd never be able to win."

"It's not about winning," Parker replied. "It's about working together. For now, at least."

Rebecca winced, while slowly closing both her fists.

"I simply realized," Parker added, "that I need to give you this chance. I need to trust you. I'm truly sorry for everything that happened to you over the years, and I know that I'm not blameless in this tale. But I'm ready to resume my role as your teacher, and I hope very much that you're willing to be my pupil again. That way, I think we can both get what we want."

"You're too kind," Rebecca purred, clenching her fists tighter as she looked once more toward the open door. "*Far* too kind."

"And there we go," Parker said, pulling the last of the chains away and letting them fall to the floor, before stepping back. "The spell is broken. You and this room are no longer hidden from the world, and the chains can no longer inhibit your powers."

"I feel that now," Rebecca whispered, with hunger in her eyes as she watched the landing. "I can go anywhere. I can *do* anything."

"I think we should start with a lesson," Parker told her. "Why don't we go downstairs and, as I suggested earlier, we can pick up right where we left off last time. I'm sure some revision will be required, but I meant every word I've said to you today. I want to teach you. I want to help you."

Rebecca opened her mouth to reply, but for a moment she was utterly mesmerized by the sight of the open door. Tears were filling her eyes now, and after a few seconds she sat up a little more.

"I can do anything," she said again, her voice barely audible as she tried to contemplate her freedom. "Are there any limits? Is there anyone who can stop me?"

"You're the only one standing in your own way," Parker said, before turning and walking toward the door. "I'll get some things ready downstairs for our next lesson. You'd like that, wouldn't you?"

"Lesson?" Rebecca replied, still clenching her fists.

Parker stopped in the doorway. Her heart was pounding, but she forced herself to keep her back turned to the bed. She hoped desperately that she was wrong, but she had an awful feeling that she knew what was about to happen.

"I'm going to teach you," she said cautiously.

"Actually," Rebecca replied, "I think it might be the other way round." She began to raise her fists, squeezing them so tight now that her cracked fingernails were digging into her palms. Blood was already starting to dribble down onto the bed. "I think *you* might be the one who needs to learn a lesson, Lydia. You've always been so high and mighty, so convinced that you're right and everyone else is wrong, so how about we start by showing you how things really work around here? You're not the only one who's had time to think over the years, and I'm pretty sure that now I know how to utterly destroy you."

"I was afraid you might say that," Parker murmured, forcing herself to keep her back turned to the girl on the bed. "Rebecca, I truly want to help you. You're very powerful but you're also weak, and you still have so much to understand. I want to help you... but I can't force you to learn."

"You've helped me more than enough already," Rebecca growled, opening her fists and aiming her bloodied palms toward the back of Parker's head. "Now it's time for me to pay you back for all your kindness!"

"Rebecca -"

"Don't even *try* to run!" Rebecca shouted angrily, as ripples of energy began to spread across her hands, threatening to burst out at any moment.

"I won't," Parker replied, turning to her. "Not now."

"Because I'll find you!" Rebecca screamed, and now the energy was growing, spreading along her arms as her eyes filled with light. "I'll always find you. And I'll burn you, Lydia! You can hide in a hundred different bodies, and I'll burn every last one of them! I'll use everything I know!"

"I'm not hiding," Parker said firmly. "I'm just -"

"I'll burn you like this!" Rebecca shouted, and in that moment the energy exploded from her hands, filling the room.

Shielding her eyes, Parker took a step back as the brightness became all-consuming. For a moment she felt the heat starting to burn her face, but that sensation quickly faded. She could hear a faint gurgling sound now, coming from the bed, and as the light faded she was able to lower her hands. Finally she looked at the bed and saw the burned figure kneeling on the center of the mattress, staring back at her with two horrified smoking eyes.

She waited, but at first Parker could only watch as Rebecca's charred body remained in place. After a few seconds the figure's mouth opened slightly, emitting a pained groan, and then flakes of burned skin began to fall from her outstretched hands like petals from a dying flower. A moment later her left arm collapsed, and now her entire body seemed to be on the verge of crumbling to nothing.

"I..." Rebecca gasped, as if she couldn't quite believe what was happening. "I... only... wanted..."

She tried to get one last word out, but instead her jaw fell away, and after a fraction of a second the bottom of her skull crumbled too. Her eyes remained visible as she blinked wildly, but then they too fell down onto the mattress as the rest of her body fell apart. Soon there was nothing left of her at all except a pile of bone and ash.

AMY CROSS

CHAPTER TWENTY-NINE

"I STILL CAN'T BELIEVE that I never noticed an entire room in the house," Colin said as he shoveled the last load of dirt onto the pile, filling the grave in the garden that now contained Rebecca's smoldering remains. "Then again, there's a lot about all of this that I don't quite get."

He paused, before turning to see that Parker was standing in the doorway, except...

Except he knew that it wasn't Parker. Not really. Although he was still struggling to wrap his head around the idea, he knew that this was someone else inhabiting Parker's body. This – he was almost able to believe now – was actually the long-dead Lydia Smith, who'd crawled out of the grave in the garden.

"If she'd just let me teach her," Parker said,

sounding exhausted as she leaned against the side of the door, "she's had been more than capable of destroying me. I'd have taught her how to do that. Instead, in her weakened state after so long left wasting away in that room, she forgot that it's not just about what you know. Anyone can amass knowledge. What's important is how..."

Her voice trailed off for a moment, and suddenly she slumped down, landing hard against the step.

"Hey!" Colin gasped, throwing the shovel aside and rushing over, trying to hold her up as she began to lean over onto one side. "Are you okay?"

"What does that mean?" she whispered.

"What does *what* mean?"

"Okay," she replied, staring back at him with an expression of incredulity. "That word seems so odd. You speak so... strangely. There's so much in this modern world that I'd love to get to know, and to experience, but..." She began to look around the garden. "I thought I could stay for a little while longer, but I don't think I have the time."

"What do you mean?" he asked.

"I used to think that I wanted to live forever," she continued, clearly struggling now to get the words out. "The truth is, eventually I would have ended up like Rebecca. I would have used my powers for bad things, or at least I would have tried to. I think that's something Old Mother Marston tried to warn me about. She was so vague, I thought I was rather stupid for not understanding at the time. I've been holding myself back, but eventually..." She paused. "Better to go out on my own terms, the way Old Mother Marston did. Better to have some control. No-one can resist these powers forever. They always corrupt. Better to... Everyone should have control over their final moments. That's only fair."

"Are you really Lydia Smith?" he asked.

She turned and stared at him, and after a moment she managed a faint smile.

"You remind me of someone," she said softly.

"Who's that?"

"Did you find out anything about dear Jimmy?"

"I think so."

"Then there's one last thing I must ask of you," she continued. "I know I have no right to ask anything at all, and I wouldn't blame you for refusing, but please..." She reached out and put a hand on the side of his arm. "I know that Jimmy must be long dead by now. Do you at least know where he's buried?"

***

The village's war memorial stood alone outside the

local church. A few people wandered past, barely even paying any attention as Colin helped a struggling Parker away from the car and over toward the small garden of remembrance in front of the memorial.

"I found his grave online," Colin said as they stopped to look at the inscription on the stone. "It's in France, in a cemetery with lots of other soldiers who died in the First World War. We could go over there and take a look."

"I'd like you to do that," Parker replied, staring in stunned awe at the memorial. "Someone should, and I don't know... I don't recall whether he had much family."

"Not according to the records." He waited for a reply. "So we'll go."

"No, not me," she said, shaking her head slightly as her knees buckled and she dropped down onto the grass. "You'll have to do it for me."

"I'm still so confused," Colin replied, crouching next to her, trying to hold her up as best he could manage. "I looked into the whole history of Styre House, and Lydia Smith, and -"

"Jimmy made sure that there were so many conflicting versions of the story," she explained, before turning as she heard a meowing sound. Spotting Smythe sneaking past a nearby gate, she began to smile. "And there's Smythe!" she exclaimed happily. "Oh, I was so mean to him sometimes! I hope he'll be able to forgive me!"

As if to answer that question, Smythe brushed against her, purring all the while. Parker reached down and stroked his side.

"I don't think he holds grudges," Colin replied.

"Oh, but he does," Parker said as her smile grew. "He holds grudges like you'd never believe. Would you mind giving me a moment alone with him?"

"With the cat?"

He waited, and then he got to his feet. Although he still didn't understand even half of what was happening, Colin figured that he needed to let Parker – or rather, Lydia – have her moment, and he told himself that he'd be able to pepper her with questions later.

"I'll just go and... check on something in the car," he said, turning and walking away. "Give me a call when you're ready to leave."

"Does he remind you of Jimmy?" Parker asked, with tears in her eyes as she continued to stroke the cat's side. "You did your job so wonderfully, Smythe. You guarded the house for more than a century. I hope you weren't too bored."

After looking up at her again, Smythe flicked his tail and pressed the side of his face against her knee.

"Well, I suppose you weren't," she said

softly. "I suppose you had all those mice to catch." She paused, and now a hint of sadness returned to her face. "You seem so strong and so alive still, but you can probably tell that I'm weakening. I'm sure I could come up with any number of Old Mother Marston's potions and spells that would extend my life, but..."

Her voice trailed off.

"But I think the time for such things has passed," she added finally, as she ran her fingers through Smythe's rich, soft fur. "It's time to go through the door that leads out of this life. Who knows? Jimmy might be waiting on the other side. Before I do that, though, I have one last task. Every witch must release her familiar eventually, and that's what I'm doing with you now."

The cat let out a brief hissing sound.

"No, I'm serious," Parker continued. "You've been a wonderful familiar, the best anyone could ever hope for, but your duty's done. You can stand down." She turned her hand around, and now she ran the back of her hand against his fur. "I have no doubt, Smythe, that you'll get yourself into more trouble. You seem to have a knack for that sort of thing. I certainly hope that you never forget me, but I also hope that you'll go out there into the world and find some new friends. You can even be someone else's familiar one day."

At this suggestion, Smythe hissed louder

than ever.

"It's not the worst idea in the world," Parker said. "You'll see. Or perhaps not. Just don't fight it if it happens. You don't seem to be weakening at all, so I have a feeling that you might be going to live for rather a long time now. I hope you'll still think of me from time to time, though." A tear ran down her cheek. "We've been a good team," she continued, and now she was really struggling to get any words out at all. "I'm sorry things weren't easier, but we managed pretty well. I love you, Smythe, and..."

She paused, before slumping down and rolling onto her back. For a moment she stared up at the gray sky, and then she let out one last long gasp before falling completely still. Her unblinking eyes watched the shifting clouds, until finally she jerked up just as Colin raced back over and Smythe hurried away.

"Are you okay?" he asked, dropping to his knees.

"I'm okay," Parker stammered, turning to him. "What... I..."

"Lydia?" he replied cautiously. "Parker? Who am I talking to right now?"

"What am I doing out here?" she asked, before reaching up and wiping away the solitary tear that had run from her eye. "The last thing I remember... I mean, I'm not sure what..."

Spotting movement, she turned just in time to see Smythe slinking past the gate and disappearing from sight. Looking around again, she tried to make sense of everything that was happening.

"The last thing I remember is being at the house," she continued. "Okay, this is really starting to freak me out." She turned to Colin. "What's going on? What happened to that thing in the garden?" She paused as a sense of dread began to spread through her chest. "Wait... where's Mum?"

CHAPTER THIRTY

ONE MONTH LATER, PARKER and Colin stood at the bottom of the steps and looked up at Styre House. Cold and empty now, the house stared back at them with unblinking windows that reflected the gray sky.

"So this is it," Parker said.

"This is it," Colin replied. "Are you sure... I mean, I understand why you want to get away and never come back, but are you sure you don't want to sell it?"

"I could use the money," she admitted, before thinking for a moment. "But no. Even though it seems like there's nothing here now, what if there's even the tiniest scrap of all that evil? Of Rebecca or whatever her name was. Of Lydia. What if it's waiting for someone else to show up, for someone who doesn't understand?"

"How would that work?"

"Maybe it thinks that we know too much," she suggested. "Maybe it's angry that it was defeated, so it wants to lurk in the shadows until someone else shows up." She rubbed the side of her head for a moment. "Sorry, sometimes I think I go on a little too much. I keep worrying that Lydia might be lingering somehow in my mind, even though deep down I know she's gone. The point is, we can never know for certain, so I guess it's best if we just play it safe."

"We've been through the place."

"I can't take that risk," she said firmly.

"Then have it bulldozed. Have someone come in with a wrecking ball and knock it all down, and then the rest can be ripped apart and taken away."

"What if the scrap's cursed?"

"Then it can be burned."

"You don't know that'd work."

"It might," he continued, struggling to contain a growing sense of exasperation. "The point is, we can find a way."

"But the land might be affected," she pointed out. "Rebecca's buried in the garden now, remember? No, I really can't take the risk. What if someone else moved in, and then they had to lose their mother the same way that I lost mine?

Whatever went on here, I just think that it should be left to rot. Maybe one day I'll get a message to say that there's been a storm and the whole place has blown away, or there'll be some random fire and the house'll burn to the ground. I'd like that. But until then, I just want to leave it alone and go away, and try not to think about it ever too often. Hopefully the police'll stop asking so many questions as well. They're obviously not willing to open their minds, so I'm pretty sure that soon they'll find some way to file it all away and forget it ever happened."

"Did you give more thought to my suggestion?"

"I'm not letting it be used by ghost-hunters!" she replied.

"I didn't say ghost-hunters, exactly," he said a little defensively. "I'm thinking more about... paranormal researchers. There are people out there who'd come and bring all sorts of equipment, and they'd be able to really go through the place and figure out if there are any ghosts. You wouldn't have to be involved, and you wouldn't even have to read their report at the end of it all."

"Are these those people who film themselves exploring haunted houses and then put it online?"

"Maybe," he said cautiously, "but... they're actual scientists."

"I'm not letting a bunch of ghost geeks go

rooting around in the house," she told him. "In fact, I don't even want anyone to know that it exists. Can you still help me to scrub all references to the place from the internet?"

"Of course, but -"

"Then it's settled," she added, cutting him off before he could come up with any more grand ideas. "No ghost-hunters."

"Is London -"

"London's a good starting point," she replied, turning to him, "but I totally get it if you want to stay here. This has all moved pretty fast."

"You don't get rid of me that easily," he countered with a faint smile. "Besides, I've already trained my replacement at the hub, and I can't really go back on that. I also want to get started on my research, and there's only so much of that I can do here. Plus we need to visit Jimmy's grave in France, and put some flowers on it. Come on, let's head to the train station. Or do you want a moment alone?"

"Here? At this place?" She turned and started walking away. "Hell, no. Although -"

Stopping suddenly, she looked back at the house, and then she turned to watch the bushes for a moment.

"Smythe?" she called out. "Hey, are you here?"

"I thought you hated that cat," Colin pointed out. "I mean, he..."

"He killed Mum," she said, finishing the sentence for him. "Yeah, I know. And I'm really not happy that we were basically used as part of a big plot to banish some deranged woman who'd been chained to a bed. But from the little that I understand, I get the feeling that Smythe was just doing his duty and protecting his mistress. I guess I can respect that." She paused, watching the shrubbery for a moment longer. "Smythe?" she shouted. "Are you still here? Can you hear me?"

"I'm sure he's long gone," Colin suggested.

"Where would he go?"

"No idea," he admitted. "Maybe he'll travel around, helping people here and there. Or killing them."

"Like some kind of satanic *Littlest Hobo*?" she asked, raising a skeptical eyebrow. "You don't seriously think that Smythe would be up for making the world a better place, do you? He's positively demonic."

"I really don't know what a semi-immortal evil cat would get up to once he's lost his familiar," he said, and then they stood for a moment watching the garden. "But there's been no sign of him since Lydia left your body, so I guess he's figured something out."

"I hope he's okay," she said, as they turned and once again made their way from the house. "I know I should want to kill the little bastard, but he was only acting on orders."

"There's one more thing I wanted to run by you," he continued. "It's a book idea, actually. It'd be a great chance to get everything written down in black and white. No rumors. No gossip. Just the cold, hard truth."

"Damn it, Colin," she sighed. "Haven't you learned anything at all about history?"

***

A gentle breeze blew through the garden of Styre House, ruffing the bushes and blowing some leaves across the grass. The breeze subsided for a few seconds, as if the sky itself was pausing for a breath, and then a slightly stronger gust blew against the garage, causing the door to loudly swing open.

Inside the house, all the rooms were empty. Most of the furniture had been left in place, and a few bloodied stains even remained as reminders of the horror that had erupted a while earlier. Some scratches were visible on the stairs, left behind by Smythe's claws, while in the formerly 'hidden' bedroom the mattress had been removed; all that remained of Rebecca's former prison was the metal frame of the bed, with some darker stains on the floorboards below.

In the master bedroom, meanwhile, a few singed spots were visible on one of the walls, although they were easy enough to miss. Alison's clothes and other belongings had been left in the various wardrobes and cupboards, and more spots of blood were dotted around on the floor. One of the windows shook slightly as it was battered by the breeze, and wind whistled briefly through a gap high up in the eaves.

Outside, a patch of disturbed soil was the only hint of the grave that now held Rebecca Barnett's remains. Deep beneath the surface, worms had already begun to break down what was left of the girl who'd spent so long chained to a bed in the house. Growing fat now, the worms burrowed their way through the soil, entirely unaware that they were eating part of someone who had once contained such power. To the worms, this material might have been anything at all; they didn't care, and they didn't even understand the concept of caring. Or power.

Meat was meat to them, regardless of who it had once been.

Above, the shrubs rustled again. Suddenly the breeze took another break, before returning and blowing a pile of rubbish away from the garage's side. Some old dead leaves blew across the soil, accompanied by a few old wrappers, and finally a half-burned page came to a rest at the top of the steps.

Having once – many years earlier – been

torn from one of Old Mother Marston's books, the page now contained only a few scraps of an old spell. Only half a dozen words could actually be read, with the rest having long since been incinerated. The page caught on a rough section at the top of the steps, before a stronger breeze blew it clean away, sending it fluttering down the steps and out onto the road, and then across the field. The page then came to a rest near some rushes, before a bird suddenly landed and began to inspect the scrap of paper.

A moment later, the bird took the page and flew away to add it to a nest where it couldn't possibly be discovered by any curious minds.

At least not for a while.

EPILOGUE

"HEAR YE, HEAR YE!" Stan Walden shouted, as he held up the ceremonial bell and shook it hard. "All ye who have gathered here, I thank you for your interest! I'm sure you're all keenly aware of the need to remember our village's remarkable past, lest we risk repeating the mistakes of our ancestors!"

A crowd had gathered on the other side of the river, while a large banner nearby bore the logo of the Almsford Historical Reenactment Society.

"On this spot in 1838," Stan continued, turning and gesturing toward the old and partially-rotten ducking stool, "the last witch in this area was drowned. Her name was Lydia Smith, and I'm sure that all of you gathered here today know her story. It might seem barbaric to us, we might abhor the way she was killed, but let us remember that sometimes people in the old days knew best. I'm sure we've all read the stories. There seem to be genuine reasons why we should all think Lydia Smith was truly a witch."

A murmur of agreement spread across the crowd, but a moment later a mobile phone began to ring.

"Would you mind silencing that?" he asked, clearly annoyed.

The ringing sound stopped.

"Everyone please check that your phones are on silent mode," he continued. "It really disrupts the mood if they ring."

He waited for a moment, giving everyone a chance to comply.

"And that is why we gather here every year," he added, as he heard footsteps approaching from his left, "to remind ourselves of our glorious past."

He stepped aside, just as two men carried a fake body up to the stool. Wearing a simple dress, with a series of stuffed pillows for its body and sporting a crudely-drawn face, the body was held up and placed on the ducking stool. The men took a moment to arrange her properly so that she appeared to be sitting upright.

"What are we to do," Stan said darkly, getting much more into character now, "when faced with the possibility that a witch lives here among us? Should we trust in the Lord to keep us safe? Should we ignore the problem? Or should we take matters into our own hands?"

"Our own hands!" a voice called out, quickly echoed by several others.

"I'd like to thank Enid and Wally Bagshaw for their work keeping the old ducking stool functional," Stan said as he stepped around to the rear of the mechanism. "If anyone wants to donate to their efforts, I'm sure you all know where to find their online fundraising page. If any of you have trouble accessing the internet, just ask a member of the committee and we'll be only too glad to assist." He reached up and took hold of the lever. "And now," he added, raising his voice, "we come to the moment of truth! If Lydia Smith is a witch, she will surely be alive once she comes out of the water. And if she is innocent, she will be dead and she can be entrusted to the arms of the Lord! Who here agrees with this test?"

A roar rang out. As a broad grin spread across his face, Stan pulled the lever and the ducking stool crashed down, quickly submerging the life-sized mannequin, just as it had submerged the struggling Lydia Smith all those years earlier.

***

"I think I'm getting a headache from all of this,"

Maurice Grundy said as he stood in the pub a short while later, along with other members of the reenactment group. "If Lydia Smith drowned in that ducking stool, doesn't that mean that she *wasn't* a witch?"

Around the room, to match the historical mood, the electric lights had all been switched off and a series of gas lamps were burning.

"You might well believe that," Stan replied, "until you learn that she supposedly rose from the dead just twenty-four hours later, and killed several more people."

"Did that really happen?"

"She killed at least thirty," Stan explained, "and then she fled to another village, where she lived until they too got tired of her antics. Then she was buried alive, and that seems to be the end of it, although she took a few more souls while she was there."

"Shocking stuff," Angela Harper said, having been listening from her spot leaning against the bar nearby. She took a sip of ale. "I'd love to go back in time and see what it was all really like. Can you imagine meeting a real witch?"

"At least the people of Almsford did the right thing," Stan said, before turning to look at the dozen or so people gathered nearby. "Everyone!" he called out. "I'd like to raise a toast! To our ancestors, from this and neighboring villages, who so bravely took on and defeated the witch Lydia Smith!"

"To our ancestors!" the others shouted merrily, clinking their glasses together before downing as much ale and wine as they could manage.

A few even burped once they were done.

"I'm going to grab something from the car," Maurice muttered, finishing his ale and setting the glass down, then heading toward the door. "It's a book on local history, I think you might find it very interesting. It's about a witch-hunter named Nykolas -"

As soon as he tried to open the door, he found that it was firmly secured. He tried again, puzzled, and then he looked out and saw the door reflected in the side of a parked car. To his surprise, he realized that someone appeared to have pushed a broom into the door's handle, keeping it from opening.

"Some silly bugger's been playing games," he said with a sigh, turning to the others. "This isn't part of the reenactment, is it?"

"Probably just kids," Stan said, heading to the back door, only to find that this too was somehow blocked. He tried a couple more times, before stepping back. "Looks like someone's tried to seal us in the pub."

"Is that a bad thing?" Archie Andrews

asked, already sounding a little worse for wear. "I wasn't planning on going anywhere anytime soon, anyway."

"It's the principle of the thing," Stan replied, "and -"

"What's that smell?" Tiff Lane said suddenly. "It's really pungent!"

For a moment, everyone looked around in silence, before finally they began to notice a large puddle spreading out from beneath the front door, gradually spreading around their feet and expanding across the entire pub.

"*Now* what's going on?" Angela asked wearily, trying to step around the puddle but quickly finding that it was everywhere. "Is it water or -"

"Petrol," Archie said, interrupting her. Reaching down, he dipped a thumb-tip into the liquid and lifted it up for a sniff. "There were some cans round the back of the building, ready for the classic car rally next week. Looks to me like some silly bugger's upended them all and it's come flooding into the pub."

"I don't like this," Maurice said, trying the front door again but finding that it was still firmly secured. "I want to get out of here."

"Everyone calm down," Stan called out. "Yes, it smells bad, but it's not poisonous or anything like that." He looked around the room. "There's no reason to -"

And then he saw him.

High up, on a shelf next to an open window, a black cat sat watching the pub's customers. Sitting next to one of the burning gas lamps, the cat stared back at the gathering with an unblinking glare that – after a few seconds – struck Stan as being in some way judgmental. Almost malicious.

"I didn't know there was a pub cat," Angela muttered.

"There isn't," Stan replied, as more and more petrol leaked out across the floor and the smell became stronger. "I think I've seen that thing around once or twice in recent days, though. It's almost like he's been scoping the place out." He stepped forward, splashing through the petrol as a couple of other men tried the front door again. "What are you up to, eh?" he asked, stopping beneath the shelf and looking up at the animal. "Weird little thing, aren't you? Are you a stray? Don't you have an owner?"

Up on the shelf, Smythe stared back down at him. A moment later, with an almost lazy sense of calm, the cat reached out with his left front paw and began to very slowly push the gas lamp toward the edge.

"Wait a minute!" Stan stammered, as he suddenly realized what would happen if the flame hit the petrol that now filled the pub. "Stop! Everyone get out of here!"

Showing no hint of a reaction at all, Smythe slowly pushed the lamp right to the edge, before stopping at the last second.

"Okay, that's better," Stan said, holding up both hands. "Everyone stay calm. The last thing we need to do is get him startled." He paused, trying to judge his moment perfectly, before slowly reaching up toward the lamp. "All we need to do is take this away," he added softly, "and then we can get out of here. As president of the Almsford Historical Reenactment Society, I really think we should -"

Smythe pushed the lamp further.

"No!" Stan hissed. "Stop!"

At the very last possible second, with the lamp teetering on the edge, Smythe stopped again.

"Nice pussycat," Stan continued. "Just... move your paw away from that lamp. Okay? You're a lovely little pussy, aren't you? You wouldn't want to hurt anyone, would you?"

With his paw still touching the side of the lamp, Smythe stared back down at him.

"Okay, you little fleabag," Stan sneered, reaching closer and closer to the lamp. "I might just tie *you* to that ducking stool later if you're not careful, and you can face the same fate as that stupid witch who -"

At that moment, Smythe pushed the lamp all the way off the shelf, before turning and racing out of the window. Behind him, flames immediately roared through the pub, and anguished cries rang out as Smythe raced across the garden. Stopping near the bushes, he turned and looked back; for a moment he purred as the growing fire filled his eyes, and then he darted out of sight as black smoke began to fill the sky.

Black smoke and screams.

THE SMYTHE TRILOGY

1. The Haunting of Styre House
2. The Curse of Bloodacre Farm
3. The Horror of Styre House

AMY CROSS

Also by Amy Cross

A CUCKOO IN WINTER

On a cold winter's day, five young girls head out into the forest.

A few hours later, six of them return.

Trapped in a nightmare, the girls frantically try to work out what's real and what's fake. They know that one of them must be an impostor, but they also remember each other. Have they been given false memories? What kind of force from the forest could possibly enter their heads and make them remember something that never happened? Or have they fallen victim to something even darker, to something more malevolent than they could ever have imagined?

Many years later, in a candlelit restaurant, the horrifying truth finally emerges... but is it too late for the surviving girls to save themselves? Is the cuckoo finally going to get exactly what it has always wanted, and what it has been waiting for since the day it first saw the five of them in the forest?

AMY CROSS

Also by Amy Cross

1689
(The Haunting of Hadlow House book 1)

All Richard Hadlow wants is a happy family and a peaceful home. Having built the perfect house deep in the Kent countryside, now all he needs is a wife. He's about to discover, however, that even the most perfectly-laid plans can go horribly and tragically wrong.

The year is 1689 and England is in the grip of turmoil. A pretender is trying to take the throne, but Richard has no interest in the affairs of his country. He only cares about finding the perfect wife and giving her a perfect life. But someone – or something – at his newly-built house has other ideas. Is Richard's new life about to be destroyed forever?

Hadlow House is brand new, but already there are strange whispers in the corridors and unexplained noises at night. Has Richard been unlucky, is his new wife simply imagining things, or is a dark secret from the past about to rise up and deliver Richard's worst nightmare? Who wins when the past and the present collide?

AMY CROSS

Also by Amy Cross

The Haunting of Nelson Street
(The Ghosts of Crowford book 1)

Crowford, a sleepy coastal town in the south of England, might seem like an oasis of calm and tranquility. Beneath the surface, however, dark secrets are waiting to claim fresh victims, and ghostly figures plot revenge.

Having finally decided to leave the hustle of London, Daisy and Richard Johnson buy two houses on Nelson Street, a picturesque street in the center of Crowford. One house is perfect and ready to move into, while the other is a fire-ravaged wreck that needs a lot of work. They figure they have plenty of time to work on the damaged house while Daisy recovers from a traumatic event.

Soon, they discover that the two houses share a common link to the past. Something awful once happened on Nelson Street, something that shook the town to its core.

Also by Amy Cross

The Revenge of the Mercy Belle
(The Ghosts of Crowford book 2)

The year is 1950, and a great tragedy has struck the town of Crowford. Three local men have been killed in a storm, after their fishing boat the Mercy Belle sank. A mysterious fourth man, however, was rescue. Nobody knows who he is, or what he was doing on the Mercy Belle... and the man has lost his memory.

Five years later, messages from the dead warn of impending doom for Crowford. The ghosts of the Mercy Belle's crew demand revenge, and the whole town is being punished. The fourth man still has no memory of his previous existence, but he's married now and living under the named Edward Smith. As Crowford's suffering continues, the locals begin to turn against him.

What really happened on the night the Mercy Belle sank? Did the fourth man cause the tragedy? And will Crowford survive if this man is not sent to meet his fate?

AMY CROSS

Also by Amy Cross

The Devil, the Witch and the Whore
(The Deal book 1)

"Leave the forest alone. Whatever's out there, just let it be. Don't make it angry."

When a horrific discovery is made at the edge of town, Sheriff James Kopperud realizes the answers he seeks might be waiting beyond in the vast forest. But everybody in the town of Deal knows that there's something out there in the forest, something that should never be disturbed. A deal was made long ago, a deal that was supposed to keep the town safe. And if he insists on investigating the murder of a local girl, James is going to have to break that deal and head out into the wilderness.

Meanwhile, James has no idea that his estranged daughter Ramsey has returned to town. Ramsey is running from something, and she thinks she can find safety in the vast tunnel system that runs beneath the forest. Before long, however, Ramsey finds herself coming face to face with creatures that hide in the shadows. One of these creatures is known as the devil, and another is known as the witch. They're both waiting for the whore to arrive, but for very different reasons. And soon Ramsey is offered a terrible deal, one that could save or destroy the entire town, and maybe even the world.

AMY CROSS

Also by Amy Cross

If You Didn't Like Me Then, You Probably Won't Like Me Now

One year ago, Sheryl and her friends did something bad. Really bad. They ritually humiliated local girl Rachel Ritter, before posting the video online for all to see. After that night, Rachel left town and was never seen again. Until now.

Late one night, Sheryl and her friends realize that Rachel's back. At first they think there's on reason to be concerned, but a series of strange events soon convince them that they need to be worried. On the outside, Rachel acts as if all is forgiven, but she's hiding a shocking secret that soon starts to have deadly consequences.

By the time they understand the full horror of Rachel's plans, Sheryl and her friends might be too late to save themselves. Is Rachel really out for revenge? What does she have in store for her tormentors? And just how far is she willing to go? Would she, for example, do something that nobody in all of human history has ever managed to achieve?

If You Didn't Like Me Then, You Probably Won't Like Me Now is a horror novel about the surprising nature of revenge, about the power of hatred, and about the future of humanity.

Also by Amy Cross

The Soul Auction

"I saw a woman on the beach. I watched her face a demon."

Thirty years after her mother's death, Alice Ashcroft is drawn back to the coastal English town of Curridge. Somebody in Curridge has been reviewing Alice's novels online, and in those reviews there have been tantalizing hints at a hidden truth. A truth that seems to be linked to her dead mother.

"Thirty years ago, there was a soul auction."

Once she reaches Curridge, Alice finds strange things happening all around her. Something attacks her car. A figure watches her on the beach at night. And when she tries to find the person who has been reviewing her books, she makes a horrific discovery.

What really happened to Alice's mother thirty years ago? Who was she talking to, just moments before dropping dead on the beach? What caused a huge rockfall that nearly tore a nearby cliff-face in half? And what sinister presence is lurking in the grounds of the local church?

AMY CROSS

Also by Amy Cross

The Ash House

Why would anyone ever return to a haunted house?

For Diane Mercer the answer is simple. She's dying of cancer, and she wants to know once and for all whether ghosts are real.

Heading home with her young son, Diane is determined to find out whether the stories are real. After all, everyone else claimed to see and hear strange things in the house over the years. Everyone except Diane had some kind of experience in the house, or in the little ash house in the yard.

As Diane explores the house where she grew up, however, her son is exploring the yard and the forest. And while his mother might be struggling to come to terms with her own impending death, Daniel Mercer is puzzled by fleeting appearances of a strange little girl who seems drawn to the ash house, and by strange, rasping coughs that he keeps hearing at night.

The Ash House is a horror novel about a woman who desperately wants to know what will happen to her when she dies, and about a boy who uncovers the shocking truth about a young girl's murder.

Also by Amy Cross

Haunted

Twenty years ago, the ghost of a dead little girl drove Sheriff Michael Blaine to his death.

Now, that same ghost is coming for his daughter.

Returning to the small town where she grew up, Alex Roberts is determined to live a normal, quiet life. For the residents of Railham, however, she's an unwelcome reminder of the town's darkest hour.

Twenty years ago, nine-year-old Mo Garvey was found brutally murdered in a nearby forest. Everyone thinks that Alex's father was responsible, but if the killer was brought to justice, why is the ghost of Mo Garvey still after revenge?

And how far will the real killer go to protect his secret, when Alex starts getting closer to the truth?

Haunted is a horror novel about a woman who has to face her past, about a town that would rather forget, and about a little girl who refuses to let death stand in her way.

AMY CROSS

Also by Amy Cross

The Curse of Wetherley House

"If you walk through that door, Evil Mary will get you."

When she agrees to visit a supposedly haunted house with an old friend, Rosie assumes she'll encounter nothing more scary than a few creaks and bumps in the night. Even the legend of Evil Mary doesn't put her off. After all, she knows ghosts aren't real. But when Mary makes her first appearance, Rosie realizes she might already be trapped.

For more than a century, Wetherley House has been cursed. A horrific encounter on a remote road in the late 1800's has already caused a chain of misery and pain for all those who live at the house. Wetherley House was abandoned long ago, after a terrible discovery in the basement, something has remained undetected within its room. And even the local children know that Evil Mary waits in the house for anyone foolish enough to walk through the front door.

Before long, Rosie realizes that her entire life has been defined by the spirit of a woman who died in agony. Can she become the first person to escape Evil Mary, or will she fall victim to the same fate as the house's other occupants?

AMY CROSS

BOOKS BY AMY CROSS

1. Dark Season: The Complete First Series (2011)
2. Werewolves of Soho (Lupine Howl book 1) (2012)
3. Werewolves of the Other London (Lupine Howl book 2) (2012)
4. Ghosts: The Complete Series (2012)
5. Dark Season: The Complete Second Series (2012)
6. The Children of Black Annis (Lupine Howl book 3) (2012)
7. Destiny of the Last Wolf (Lupine Howl book 4) (2012)
8. Asylum (The Asylum Trilogy book 1) (2012)
9. Dark Season: The Complete Third Series (2013)
10. Devil's Briar (2013)
11. Broken Blue (The Broken Trilogy book 1) (2013)
12. The Night Girl (2013)
13. Days 1 to 4 (Mass Extinction Event book 1) (2013)
14. Days 5 to 8 (Mass Extinction Event book 2) (2013)
15. The Library (The Library Chronicles book 1) (2013)
16. American Coven (2013)
17. Werewolves of Sangreth (Lupine Howl book 5) (2013)
18. Broken White (The Broken Trilogy book 2) (2013)
19. Grave Girl (Grave Girl book 1) (2013)
20. Other People's Bodies (2013)
21. The Shades (2013)
22. The Vampire's Grave and Other Stories (2013)
23. Darper Danver: The Complete First Series (2013)
24. The Hollow Church (2013)
25. The Dead and the Dying (2013)
26. Days 9 to 16 (Mass Extinction Event book 3) (2013)
27. The Girl Who Never Came Back (2013)
28. Ward Z (The Ward Z Series book 1) (2013)
29. Journey to the Library (The Library Chronicles book 2) (2014)
30. The Vampires of Tor Cliff Asylum (2014)
31. The Family Man (2014)
32. The Devil's Blade (2014)
33. The Immortal Wolf (Lupine Howl book 6) (2014)
34. The Dying Streets (Detective Laura Foster book 1) (2014)
35. The Stars My Home (2014)
36. The Ghost in the Rain and Other Stories (2014)
37. Ghosts of the River Thames (The Robinson Chronicles book 1) (2014)
38. The Wolves of Cur'eath (2014)
39. Days 46 to 53 (Mass Extinction Event book 4) (2014)
40. The Man Who Saw the Face of the World (2014)
41. The Art of Dying (Detective Laura Foster book 2) (2014)
42. Raven Revivals (Grave Girl book 2) (2014)

43. Arrival on Thaxos (Dead Souls book 1) (2014)
44. Birthright (Dead Souls book 2) (2014)
45. A Man of Ghosts (Dead Souls book 3) (2014)
46. The Haunting of Hardstone Jail (2014)
47. A Very Respectable Woman (2015)
48. Better the Devil (2015)
49. The Haunting of Marshall Heights (2015)
50. Terror at Camp Everbee (The Ward Z Series book 2) (2015)
51. Guided by Evil (Dead Souls book 4) (2015)
52. Child of a Bloodied Hand (Dead Souls book 5) (2015)
53. Promises of the Dead (Dead Souls book 6) (2015)
54. Days 54 to 61 (Mass Extinction Event book 5) (2015)
55. Angels in the Machine (The Robinson Chronicles book 2) (2015)
56. The Curse of Ah-Qal's Tomb (2015)
57. Broken Red (The Broken Trilogy book 3) (2015)
58. The Farm (2015)
59. Fallen Heroes (Detective Laura Foster book 3) (2015)
60. The Haunting of Emily Stone (2015)
61. Cursed Across Time (Dead Souls book 7) (2015)
62. Destiny of the Dead (Dead Souls book 8) (2015)
63. The Death of Jennifer Kazakos (Dead Souls book 9) (2015)
64. Alice Isn't Well (Death Herself book 1) (2015)
65. Annie's Room (2015)
66. The House on Everley Street (Death Herself book 2) (2015)
67. Meds (The Asylum Trilogy book 2) (2015)
68. Take Me to Church (2015)
69. Ascension (Demon's Grail book 1) (2015)
70. The Priest Hole (Nykolas Freeman book 1) (2015)
71. Eli's Town (2015)
72. The Horror of Raven's Briar Orphanage (Dead Souls book 10) (2015)
73. The Witch of Thaxos (Dead Souls book 11) (2015)
74. The Rise of Ashalla (Dead Souls book 12) (2015)
75. Evolution (Demon's Grail book 2) (2015)
76. The Island (The Island book 1) (2015)
77. The Lighthouse (2015)
78. The Cabin (The Cabin Trilogy book 1) (2015)
79. At the Edge of the Forest (2015)
80. The Devil's Hand (2015)
81. The 13th Demon (Demon's Grail book 3) (2016)
82. After the Cabin (The Cabin Trilogy book 2) (2016)
83. The Border: The Complete Series (2016)
84. The Dead Ones (Death Herself book 3) (2016)
85. A House in London (2016)
86. Persona (The Island book 2) (2016)

87. Battlefield (Nykolas Freeman book 2) (2016)
88. Perfect Little Monsters and Other Stories (2016)
89. The Ghost of Shapley Hall (2016)
90. The Blood House (2016)
91. The Death of Addie Gray (2016)
92. The Girl With Crooked Fangs (2016)
93. Last Wrong Turn (2016)
94. The Body at Auercliff (2016)
95. The Printer From Hell (2016)
96. The Dog (2016)
97. The Nurse (2016)
98. The Haunting of Blackwych Grange (2016)
99. Twisted Little Things and Other Stories (2016)
100. The Horror of Devil's Root Lake (2016)
101. The Disappearance of Katie Wren (2016)
102. B&B (2016)
103. The Bride of Ashbyrn House (2016)
104. The Devil, the Witch and the Whore (The Deal Trilogy book 1) (2016)
105. The Ghosts of Lakeforth Hotel (2016)
106. The Ghost of Longthorn Manor and Other Stories (2016)
107. Laura (2017)
108. The Murder at Skellin Cottage (Jo Mason book 1) (2017)
109. The Curse of Wetherley House (2017)
110. The Ghosts of Hexley Airport (2017)
111. The Return of Rachel Stone (Jo Mason book 2) (2017)
112. Haunted (2017)
113. The Vampire of Downing Street and Other Stories (2017)
114. The Ash House (2017)
115. The Ghost of Molly Holt (2017)
116. The Camera Man (2017)
117. The Soul Auction (2017)
118. The Abyss (The Island book 3) (2017)
119. Broken Window (The House of Jack the Ripper book 1) (2017)
120. In Darkness Dwell (The House of Jack the Ripper book 2) (2017)
121. Cradle to Grave (The House of Jack the Ripper book 3) (2017)
122. The Lady Screams (The House of Jack the Ripper book 4) (2017)
123. A Beast Well Tamed (The House of Jack the Ripper book 5) (2017)
124. Doctor Charles Grazier (The House of Jack the Ripper book 6) (2017)
125. The Raven Watcher (The House of Jack the Ripper book 7) (2017)
126. The Final Act (The House of Jack the Ripper book 8) (2017)
127. Stephen (2017)
128. The Spider (2017)
129. The Mermaid's Revenge (2017)
130. The Girl Who Threw Rocks at the Devil (2018)

AMY CROSS

131. Friend From the Internet (2018)
132. Beautiful Familiar (2018)
133. One Night at a Soul Auction (2018)
134. 16 Frames of the Devil's Face (2018)
135. The Haunting of Caldgrave House (2018)
136. Like Stones on a Crow's Back (The Deal Trilogy book 2) (2018)
137. Room 9 and Other Stories (2018)
138. The Gravest Girl of All (Grave Girl book 3) (2018)
139. Return to Thaxos (Dead Souls book 13) (2018)
140. The Madness of Annie Radford (The Asylum Trilogy book 3) (2018)
141. The Haunting of Briarwych Church (Briarwych book 1) (2018)
142. I Just Want You To Be Happy (2018)
143. Day 100 (Mass Extinction Event book 6) (2018)
144. The Horror of Briarwych Church (Briarwych book 2) (2018)
145. The Ghost of Briarwych Church (Briarwych book 3) (2018)
146. Lights Out (2019)
147. Apocalypse (The Ward Z Series book 3) (2019)
148. Days 101 to 108 (Mass Extinction Event book 7) (2019)
149. The Haunting of Daniel Bayliss (2019)
150. The Purchase (2019)
151. Harper's Hotel Ghost Girl (Death Herself book 4) (2019)
152. The Haunting of Aldburn House (2019)
153. Days 109 to 116 (Mass Extinction Event book 8) (2019)
154. Bad News (2019)
155. The Wedding of Rachel Blaine (2019)
156. Dark Little Wonders and Other Stories (2019)
157. The Music Man (2019)
158. The Vampire Falls (Three Nights of the Vampire book 1) (2019)
159. The Other Ann (2019)
160. The Butcher's Husband and Other Stories (2019)
161. The Haunting of Lannister Hall (2019)
162. The Vampire Burns (Three Nights of the Vampire book 2) (2019)
163. Days 195 to 202 (Mass Extinction Event book 9) (2019)
164. Escape From Hotel Necro (2019)
165. The Vampire Rises (Three Nights of the Vampire book 3) (2019)
166. Ten Chimes to Midnight: A Collection of Ghost Stories (2019)
167. The Strangler's Daughter (2019)
168. The Beast on the Tracks (2019)
169. The Haunting of the King's Head (2019)
170. I Married a Serial Killer (2019)
171. Your Inhuman Heart (2020)
172. Days 203 to 210 (Mass Extinction Event book 10) (2020)
173. The Ghosts of David Brook (2020)
174. Days 349 to 356 (Mass Extinction Event book 11) (2020)

175. The Horror at Criven Farm (2020)
176. Mary (2020)
177. The Middlewych Experiment (Chaos Gear Annie book 1) (2020)
178. Days 357 to 364 (Mass Extinction Event book 12) (2020)
179. Day 365: The Final Day (Mass Extinction Event book 13) (2020)
180. The Haunting of Hathaway House (2020)
181. Don't Let the Devil Know Your Name (2020)
182. The Legend of Rinth (2020)
183. The Ghost of Old Coal House (2020)
184. The Root (2020)
185. I'm Not a Zombie (2020)
186. The Ghost of Annie Close (2020)
187. The Disappearance of Lonnie James (2020)
188. The Curse of the Langfords (2020)
189. The Haunting of Nelson Street (The Ghosts of Crowford 1) (2020)
190. Strange Little Horrors and Other Stories (2020)
191. The House Where She Died (2020)
192. The Revenge of the Mercy Belle (The Ghosts of Crowford 2) (2020)
193. The Ghost of Crowford School (The Ghosts of Crowford book 3) (2020)
194. The Haunting of Hardlocke House (2020)
195. The Cemetery Ghost (2020)
196. You Should Have Seen Her (2020)
197. The Portrait of Sister Elsa (The Ghosts of Crowford book 4) (2021)
198. The House on Fisher Street (2021)
199. The Haunting of the Crowford Hoy (The Ghosts of Crowford 5) (2021)
200. Trill (2021)
201. The Horror of the Crowford Empire (The Ghosts of Crowford 6) (2021)
202. Out There (The Ted Armitage Trilogy book 1) (2021)
203. The Nightmare of Crowford Hospital (The Ghosts of Crowford 7) (2021)
204. Twist Valley (The Ted Armitage Trilogy book 2) (2021)
205. The Great Beyond (The Ted Armitage Trilogy book 3) (2021)
206. The Haunting of Edward House (2021)
207. The Curse of the Crowford Grand (The Ghosts of Crowford 8) (2021)
208. How to Make a Ghost (2021)
209. The Ghosts of Crossley Manor (The Ghosts of Crowford 9) (2021)
210. The Haunting of Matthew Thorne (2021)
211. The Siege of Crowford Castle (The Ghosts of Crowford 10) (2021)
212. Daisy: The Complete Series (2021)
213. Bait (Bait book 1) (2021)
214. Origin (Bait book 2) (2021)
215. Heretic (Bait book 3) (2021)
216. Anna's Sister (2021)
217. The Haunting of Quist House (The Rose Files 1) (2021)
218. The Haunting of Crowford Station (The Ghosts of Crowford 11) (2022)

AMY CROSS

219. The Curse of Rosie Stone (2022)
220. The First Order (The Chronicles of Sister June book 1) (2022)
221. The Second Veil (The Chronicles of Sister June book 2) (2022)
222. The Graves of Crowford Rise (The Ghosts of Crowford 12) (2022)
223. Dead Man: The Resurrection of Morton Kane (2022)
224. The Third Beast (The Chronicles of Sister June book 3) (2022)
225. The Legend of the Crossley Stag (The Ghosts of Crowford 13) (2022)
226. One Star (2022)
227. The Ghost in Room 119 (2022)
228. The Fourth Shadow (The Chronicles of Sister June book 4) (2022)
229. The Soldier Without a Past (Dead Souls book 14) (2022)
230. The Ghosts of Marsh House (2022)
231. Wax: The Complete Series (2022)
232. The Phantom of Crowford Theatre (The Ghosts of Crowford 14) (2022)
233. The Haunting of Hurst House (Mercy Willow book 1) (2022)
234. Blood Rains Down From the Sky (The Deal Trilogy book 3) (2022)
235. The Spirit on Sidle Street (Mercy Willow book 2) (2022)
236. The Ghost of Gower Grange (Mercy Willow book 3) (2022)
237. The Curse of Clute Cottage (Mercy Willow book 4) (2022)
238. The Haunting of Anna Jenkins (Mercy Willow book 5) (2023)
239. The Death of Mercy Willow (Mercy Willow book 6) (2023)
240. Angel (2023)
241. The Eyes of Maddy Park (2023)
242. If You Didn't Like Me Then, You Probably Won't Like Me Now (2023)
243. The Terror of Torfork Tower (Mercy Willow 7) (2023)
244. The Phantom of Payne Priory (Mercy Willow 8) (2023)
245. The Devil on Davis Drive (Mercy Willow 9) (2023)
246. The Haunting of the Ghost of Tom Bell (Mercy Willow 10) (2023)
247. The Other Ghost of Gower Grange (Mercy Willow 11) (2023)
248. The Haunting of Olive Atkins (Mercy Willow 12) (2023)
249. The End of Marcy Willow (Mercy Willow 13) (2023)
250. The Last Haunted House on Mars and Other Stories (2023)
251. 1689 (The Haunting of Hadlow House 1) (2023)
252. 1722 (The Haunting of Hadlow House 2) (2023)
253. 1775 (The Haunting of Hadlow House 3) (2023)
254. The Terror of Crowford Carnival (The Ghosts of Crowford 15) (2023)
255. 1800 (The Haunting of Hadlow House 4) (2023)
256. 1837 (The Haunting of Hadlow House 5) (2023)
257. 1885 (The Haunting of Hadlow House 6) (2023)
258. 1901 (The Haunting of Hadlow House 7) (2023)
259. 1918 (The Haunting of Hadlow House 8) (2023)
260. The Secret of Adam Grey (The Ghosts of Crowford 16) (2023)
261. 1926 (The Haunting of Hadlow House 9) (2023)
262. 1939 (The Haunting of Hadlow House 10) (2023)

263. The Fifth Tomb (The Chronicles of Sister June 5) (2023)
264. 1966 (The Haunting of Hadlow House 11) (2023)
265. 1999 (The Haunting of Hadlow House 12) (2023)
266. The Hauntings of Mia Rush (2023)
267. 2024 (The Haunting of Hadlow House 13) (2024)
268. The Sixth Window (The Chronicles of Sister June 6) (2024)
269. Little Miss Dead (The Horrors of Sobolton 1) (2024)
270. Swan Territory (The Horrors of Sobolton 2) (2024)
271. Dead Widow Road (The Horrors of Sobolton 3) (2024)
272. The Haunting of Stryke Brothers (The Ghosts of Crowford 17) (2024)
273. In a Lonely Grave (The Horrors of Sobolton 4) (2024)
274. Electrification (The Horrors of Sobolton 5) (2024)
275. Man on the Moon (The Horrors of Sobolton 6) (2024)
276. The Haunting of Styre House (The Smythe Trilogy 1) (2024)
277. The Curse of Bloodacre Farm (The Smythe Trilogy 2) (2024)
278. The Horror of Styre House (The Smythe Trilogy 3) (2024)

AMY CROSS

For more information, visit:

www.amycross.com

AMY CROSS

Printed in Great Britain
by Amazon